# KISS ME GOODNIGHT IN ROME

THE COLLEGE PACT SERIES

GINA AZZI

*Kiss Me Goodnight in Rome*

Copyright © 2019 by Gina Azzi

All rights reserved.

This is a work of fiction. Names, characters, businesses, places, events, locales, and incidents are either the products of the author's imagination or used in a fictitious manner. Any resemblance to actual persons, living or dead, or actual events is purely coincidental.

# A NOTE ABOUT KISS ME GOODNIGHT IN ROME

*Kiss Me Goodnight in Rome* is a coming-of-age, contemporary romance that includes sensitive themes. It is intended for mature audiences.

---

*Kiss Me Goodnight in Rome* was formerly published as part of The Senior Semester Series. It has been re-edited and revamped with new content and a fresh look.

## THE COLLEGE PACT SERIES

Four best friends.
Four sexy athletes.
Four hot romances.
One college pact!

**Coming Summer 2019**
*The Last First Game* (Lila's Story) - June 4, 2019
*Kiss Me Goodnight in Rome* (Mia's Story) -
June 20, 2019
*All the While* (Maura's Story) - July 16, 2019
*Me + You* (Emma's Story) - August 14, 2019

AUGUST

# PROLOGUE

## Mia

"What about this?" I ask my friends, smoothing my hands over my hips.

Maura, Lila, and Emma lounge around my bedroom in New York, assessing my wardrobe and offering advice. I study my reflection, biting my lip. The dress is black, knee-length, with a square neckline and thick straps. It's classy yet understated. I wore it to the Junior-Senior dance showcase during my sophomore year at McShain University.

Lila tosses her long blond waves over her shoulder, her eyes crinkling. "You're kidding me, right?"

"What's wrong with it? Oh, jeez, is the neckline too low?" I tug it up higher.

"You look like you're going to a funeral." Emma points at me.

Glancing at Maura, she nods.

Epic fail. How the hell am I supposed to embrace the college pact if I can't even look the part? I've never stepped out of my comfort zone before and after months of watching my life implode, I'm ready for a change. I need an adventure, an experience…something to remind me that I'm going to be okay.

"Don't question Emma, Mia. She may not be right about everything," Lila says, blowing a kiss in Emma's direction, "but when it comes to fashion, take her advice and run with it."

"Mia, you're going to Italy, the epicenter of fashion. Embrace it. Wear colors and try new things. Rome is not some stuffy ballet theater." Emma stands next to me. Squeezing my shoulder in the reflection of the mirror, she grins, "It's … well, it's everything."

"What does that even mean?" Maura raises a sculpted eyebrow.

"It means that this," Emma indicates my black dress, "isn't going to cut it for Rome. Luckily I brought some options. Nothing too crazy," she clarifies as I open my mouth to protest, "just a few staples." She moves to her overnight bag, pulling out an armful of clothing.

"Yes!" Lila claps her hands. "This is perfect for the pact, Mia." Lila takes some articles of clothing from Emma, spreading them out on my bed. "You promised." She adds as if I could forget an agreement I made only hours ago.

"Date tall, dark, and handsomes," Maura rolls her eyes as she references Lila's favorite topic: boys.

"Obviously. And have an epic senior year. Being adventurous, embracing the moment, making sure we have no regrets." Lila summarizes. "We all agreed."

We did all agree. We made a pact to have a wild, adventurous, exciting senior year – stepping out of our comfort zones, pushing the envelope, bending the rules. We raised our glasses and drank to this new journey.

Except I'm the ultimate rule follower and the thought of

being wild gives me hives. The fear of moving to Rome tomorrow morning for my study abroad is thick in my throat, causing my tongue to stick. Thoughts ricochet in my mind, rendering me unable to respond to Emma's fashion suggestions as she holds up her basic staples or meet Lila's eyes as she chatters about Italian men and Ferraris.

Except I need this pact. I need this change. For too long, I've been stuck. Now, I'm twenty-one-years-old and I don't know how to flirt, mingle, and make small talk. I have no clue how to fill my time after so many years adhering to my strict ballet schedule. I've never traded study sessions in the library for nights out with the girls.

I understand discipline, dedication, and organization. Without my friends, without ballet and the familiarity of McShain's campus, I'm not sure I know how to…be.

But God, do I want to.

Maura offers a sympathetic smile. "I'm really proud of you for doing this, for being brave. And I know your mom is looking down on you smiling that you're taking this trip. Trust me, it's going to be worth it."

An unexpected swell of emotion bubbles in my throat. *I can do this. I can be a person who learns how to have free time. And enjoy it. Can't I?*

"And your black dress is practical." Maura adds.

"Thanks," my fingers fidget over the lines of my dress. In the mirror, my straight brown hair falls limply to my shoulders. Sucking in my stomach, it barely moves. My thick, fleshy thighs expand before my eyes. So gross.

My face is pasty pale with two dull, void eyes staring back. All sparkle vanished after I lost ballet, which snuffed out my future dreams and shattered my heart. Closing my eyes so I don't have to stare at all my imperfections simultaneously, I count to ten.

But when I open them, my bland expression, bloated stomach, and boring black dress are still there.

*Yes, I need this. It's time for a change. A life makeover.*

"It's the new you!" Emma exclaims, reading my thoughts. She unzips the back of my dress and it slides down my body, pooling around my feet like a waterfall. "Seriously, Mia, if I had your figure, I would definitely flaunt it a bit more. You're one of the lucky ones, everything looks amazing on you. So do us thicker girls a favor and slut it up a bit. Here, put this one on." She hands me a short, olive green sweater dress. "I stole it from my sister, so there's a tiny chance it will actually fit you and not just hang off your limbs."

Pulling the dress over my head, I smooth it down my frame.

"Pair it with tights and these boots." Emma holds up a pair of brown leather boots with a chunky heel. "They're comfy. Swear it." She tosses the boots into my open suitcase.

"Oh, you are going to turn heads and break hearts, Mia Petrella!" Lila shouts, picking up a bottle of wine she deposited on my desk hours ago. Digging into her purse, her hand exits with a corkscrew. Opening the bottle, she takes a long swig and passes it to me. "I bet you even lose your virginity."

Rolling my eyes, I lift a hand to stop my friends before they can launch into —

"It's not that there's anything wrong with being a virgin." Emma says slowly.

"Not at all. It's just, who could be better than an Italian for her first time?" Lila asks as if there is no possible comparison.

"True." Emma agrees.

Maura swipes the bottle from my hand and chugs. Her newly discovered appreciation for wine, or alcohol in general, is evident when she smacks her lips. "I'm kind of jealous you're going to drink this nectar from the gods like the rest of us drink water. If you do decide to cash in your V-card, make sure you drink several bottles first."

"Maura!" Emma tugs on Maura's long, curly hair and shakes her head. Looking at me, she grins, "She's exaggerating. While the first time may be uncomfortable, it's not like, excruciatingly painful."

"Guys, it's fine. Honestly, I need this. The pact, the adventure, the hot guys. I'm turning over a new leaf. Mia Petrella, the ballerina, is done. It's time to invent a new me."

"Hell yeah, girl! You are going to slay. I would do the first man who called me *bella*," Lila places her hand over her heart. "You look hot. I like this color on you."

"There's more!" Emma holds up a pile of sweaters, depositing them in my suitcase.

"Rome is going to be amazing. Think of all the sexy Italian men you're going to meet. I bet they're all tall, dark, and handsome." Lila sighs, twirling around my bedroom.

"I never thought I'd say this, Li, but I'm ready to meet them all." I hold up the wine bottle, tip it back, and take a large gulp.

Liquid courage.

I'm going to embrace this.

Ciao a Roma.

# 1

## LORENZO

S leek. Fast. Fierce.

My brand-new baby, a Maserati GranTurismo, rips to life as sweat beads along my hairline. Narrowing my gaze on the finish line, I clench the steering wheel, ignoring the flash of yellow that hovers in my peripheral vision.

*Come on, Enzo. You got this.*

Saliva pools in my mouth, my body tensing, my mind momentarily blank, as I cross the finish line.

Beautiful women, clad in skimpy crop tops and tiny shorts drape across the hood of my car as I come to a stop. That's when my thoughts come barreling back, tripping over each other for my attention.

*Did I win?*

*Did I lose my edge?*

*Could I qualify for the F1 Circuit again?*

My body hums with adrenaline, my heart rate spiking as I look around, wild for confirmation.

*Did I fucking win?*

It's not about the money; I don't need it. Nor do I need the props and the credit. Nope, I need to know, for myself, that I still own this sport. That I haven't gone soft; that I can still beat out the competition. And while this isn't the professional circuit I'm used to, I'll race digs all night, every night, and beat all these fuckers, until I'm racing for real again.

"You won." My best friend Sandro pulls open my car door, looking over his shoulder. "Carabineri have been tipped off. You need to go." He hustles me out of my car.

"Oh, hell yeah!" I glance skyward, sending up a silent thank you.

"Enzo, you can't get arrested again." The seriousness of Sandro's tone sobers me. "Go with Alessandra; she'll take care of you." He flips his chin toward a slamming brunette with bright hazel eyes.

Nodding, I toss him my car keys, knowing he'll sort out my mess. We've been friends a long time, more like brothers, and if Sandro is telling me I need to hustle, then I need to leave.

"Sweet race, Enzo." Alessandra purrs, biting the corner of her mouth.

"What are you doing tonight?"

"You." She quirks an eyebrow, trailing a finger along my chest, down my stomach, her hand gripping my belt.

The corners of my mouth curl into a grin. Isn't she beautiful? Sure, too much makeup and dressed to garner the attention of every male in a thirty-kilometer radius, but beautiful. Curves and dips in all the right places, stunning eyes, perfect tits, and, the best part of all, no interest in small talk.

"I need to get lost. Your place or mine?"

"Mine."

"Va bene. You drive." I palm the swell of her ass as she leads me toward her car.

In the distance, sirens ring out. Damn police. Who tipped

them off this time? Sandro's right, I can't get arrested again; last time nearly broke Mama's heart.

"You were really great tonight." Alessandra flips the ignition of her ride, pulling onto a side street, in the opposite direction of sirens and flashing lights. "This stronzo don't stand a chance against you, an F1 driver."

"Not doing that anymore, babe."

"You'll be back, Enzo."

"Yeah? What makes you so sure?" My tone is sharper than I intend, and I hate that I'm desperate for her words, desperate for reassurance that I'll race again. Even from a woman I'll never see again after tonight.

"You're too ambitious. And arrogant."

Barking out a laugh, I nod. "Pull over."

A ghost of a smiles shadows her mouth as she parks on a side street. Her lips are painted Ferrari red, her eyes already hooded. Swiping her tongue along her bottom lip, she turns to face me. Slowly, she crosses her arms and lifts her tiny shirt over her head. Her breasts spill out, full and heavy, two pert nipples staring at me like headlights.

"Like what you see?" she teases.

"Stop talking." I palm her left breast, gripping her waist with my right hand and pulling her forward until she straddles me in the passenger seat. Lowering the seat, I lean back as she grinds into me, her long hair falling forward like a curtain.

"You won't forget this, Enzo. You won't forget me." She whispers, dipping her head, her fingers flicking open the button on my jeans.

But I've already forgotten her name.

Instead I hold onto the sensations rolling through my body, focus on the physical, and let her finish my night off on a high.

———

"Lorenzo Barca!"

Loud. Too loud. Why so much shouting after such an incredible night?

"What the hell?" I shout, bolting up in bed, as cold water shocks my system. "That feels like ice!"

"It should. It's ice water." Mama crosses her arms, glaring at me.

"Buon giorno, Mama."

"It's not a very good morning, Lorenzo. Do you know why?"

I shake my head, my stomach sinking, because I have a few guesses.

"Captain Dinofrio just left."

I wince.

"Street racing! Again? You know better. Why are you doing this to me? Your Papa passed only six months ago and if he knew what you were putting me through, he would roll over in his grave."

"Mama, I —"

"I don't want to hear it. It's my fault; I've coddled you. I've been too soft on you when I should have been stricter."

"Mama, it's —"

"I know losing Papa devastated you. It's devastated all of us. But, this, Lorenzo," she holds her hands out wide, her Italian taking on the dialect of her childhood, "the drunk driving, the reckless partying, all the women, this is why you lost all your qualifying races. This is why you are not competing on the F1 circuit this year. This is on you."

Her words rattle around my head like ping pong balls.

She's right; it is my fault that I lost my career. I only have myself to blame.

Anger unravels in my blood, traveling through my veins like smoke. All I need is one word, one look, to spark the match that will initiate a wildfire.

Mama holds up a hand, halting my outburst. "You're lucky it was Captain Dinofrio and he's looking the other way. But, you need to change your ways. And so, I will help you. Starting today, you will begin working at Angelina's."

Groaning, I flop back onto my bed, screwing my eyes closed.

"Five or six shifts a week, depending on how busy we are. Although, I anticipate full tables now that the academic year is beginning. You know Angelina's is a favorite study spot for the foreign exchange students so maybe even seven shifts a week. It's time for you to start taking part in this family's business. I'll see you there for lunch. Bring an apron."

My bedroom door slams behind her.

Scrubbing a hand over my face, the scruff lining my jaw prickles my fingers. Sighing, I shake my head to clear it and stand up, my stomach revolting. Took too many shots after I screwed Alessandra.

"The prodigal son returns." My sister's voice is laced with sarcasm.

"What do you want Claudia?"

"Good morning to you too." She smiles sweetly from my doorway, a new Valentino purse hanging off her wrist as she studies her manicure. Glancing up, she winces. "You look awful."

"I'm hungover."

"Out with Sandro?"

I nod. "After a dig last night, we hit some bars. Ended up at a casino in Sanremo."

"It's amazing you're still alive sometimes."

"I won."

"I figured; that's why I didn't ask."

I gesture for my sister to leave and she chuckles.

"What are you still doing here? Don't you have a party to plan or whatever it is you do with your time?" I ask after a beat.

A frown twists Claudia's lips. "This was a stupid idea." She murmurs to herself, backing out of my room.

"Claudia, wait." I pinch the bridge of my nose for patience. "What's going on?"

She glares at me for a long moment before sighing. "I heard Mama on the phone with Zio Benito."

My head snaps up, my eyes boring into hers. "Are you sure?"

She nods.

"A hundred percent sure?"

"Yes. This is bad, isn't it?"

My heart thumps in my ears, causing the nausea in my stomach to intensify. Anything to do with Zio Benito is bad news. Always. "Real bad."

"Has Giuseppe or Rafaello or anyone mentioned anything when you met with them?" Claudia asks, referencing Papa's accountant and lawyer.

Squinting, I try and recall our recent conversations. There was something about ledgers being fudged, inflation, and... damn, I need to stop inhaling the Negronis before business meetings. I shrug.

"Just, ask around, okay?" Claudia worries her bottom lip between her teeth and I nod, softening toward her.

*When did things grow so hostile between us?*

"Sure, Claudia."

"Good luck at Angelina's; it won't be too bad with all the study abroad girls arriving."

Snorting, I nod. "Small miracles."

"I guess so."

---

WALKING into Angelina's kitchen before the lunch service, Mama glances up from her station of chopping vegetables.

"Ciao, caro," she greets me. "You're early."

"Mama." I drop a kiss to her cheek.

Patting my face, she turns back to her work, but not before I note the exhaustion that hugs her blue eyes and wisps of grey hair that escape her bun. Guilt churns in my stomach and I bite back the harsh complaints on my tongue.

Blowing out a breath, I reach around Mama, don a clean apron, and chop tomatoes. Soon, we're chopping in unison.

"Like old times, no?"

"You used to be a good little helper, Lorenzo."

Simona, our hostess, breezes into the kitchen, avoiding my gaze but speaking to me from the corner of her mouth. "The table of women on the patio would like a bottle of red wine."

"Got it."

Red stains her cheeks as she cuts Mama a look and darts out of the kitchen.

"Don't kiss any more of my girls, Lorenzo. I can't keep training new ones. And Simona, she is good at her job."

Snorting, I hold my palms up to Mama but she shakes her head and focuses on the vegetables.

Simona and I slept together a month ago; it was a one-night thing. Too much wine. She had just broken up with some stronzo; I was bored. Still, her blushing bride routine whenever she sees me is entertaining.

Grabbing a bottle of our house red, made at our family

vineyard in Tuscany, I stack some glasses and head out to the patio.

"Lorenzo," Mama's voice stops me. "Help me with this restaurant. Help me rebuild it the way my father did. Work here because you want to, because you care about our family's legacy."

I turn toward her, keeping my face impassive.

Mama raises her eyebrows. "Do this for me. Focus on family, on hard work. And next season, I bet you qualify again."

"You don't know that, Mama."

"You weren't in the right frame of mind last season. You still aren't. Come back to basics, Lorenzo. Come back to family and you will see; your fortune will change."

# 2

# MIA

E mma was right.

Rome is everything.

The cobblestone streets, the scent of fresh pizza dough, the simultaneous existence of ancient ruins and modern technology surround me. So much culture and history and beauty packed into every step.

I can't believe I'm really here.

But here I am. Standing in the center of a large piazza, Campo de' Fiori, looking up at a statue of Giordano Bruno, the free-thinking friar burned to death in 1600.

Pulling out my cell phone to check the time, I grin at the slew of messages lighting up my screen.

*Dad: Did you land yet? Message me when you're there. Be careful, Mia. Love you.*

*Emma: Buon giorno bitch. Send me photos.*

*Maura: Fav gelato? I'm awaiting an update…*

*Lila: Miss you already! Any pact news i.e. have you met an Italiano?*

*Me (to everyone): I just arrived a few hours ago! Rome is*

*amazing. I'm still waiting to meet my host family. Going to grab an espresso now. XO*

Since I arrived in the middle of the day, my host parents, Gianluca and Paola Franchetti, are at work. They left keys for me at the university so I could stow my luggage at the apartment before exploring Rome.

Meandering down a side street, I pause at a cute restaurant with an outdoor patio. Angelina's. Sitting down at a table, I flip through the menu, scanning the incredible pizza and pasta dishes I'll never order.

"Ciao." His voice is husky, smooth but commanding, like a series of fouetté turns.

Glancing up, I freeze. Because servers in America don't look like this guy. Hell, models don't look like him. Blue eyes, the color of the Mediterranean Sea, meet mine. He checks every box for one of Lila's tall, dark, and handsomes. Standing over six feet tall, his dark hair curls slightly behind his ears and over the collar of his shirt. His jawline is as sculpted as Michelangelo's David, with a slight shadow dusting his cheeks and chin.

He's devilishly handsome and I blush from his gaze alone.

Except he's not smiling or winking or being charming at all.

Instead, he's glaring at me, his eyes glacial, his jaw clenched; he may as well be carved from marble. A sigh falls from his full lips, irritated. "Cosa vorremo ordinare?"

He glances over his shoulder, his eyes zeroing in on a beautiful woman seated at another table, surrounded by her equally beautiful friends. She crosses one tanned leg over the other, her skirt riding up.

He turns back to me, impatience rippling over his expression.

My breath lodges in my throat, embarrassment crawling up my neck, threatening to choke me. What did he ask me? And why is he so angry to take my order? I know I don't look like the Victoria's Secret Angel sitting at table three but I'm a perfectly nice —

"What would you like to order?" He switches to English, his tone hard.

My mouth falls open, but no words follow.

*Get it together, Mia. You want an espresso. Or a latte? Caffeine, you want caffeine!*

"Lorenzo! Another bottle of wine." The beauty queen raises an empty bottle and shakes it at him.

Lorenzo turns away from me again, gesturing that he'll be a moment. "I'll be back. Figure out what you want." He spits at me, turning to the other table. Chatting with the woman and her friends, his eyes dart back to me. Their Italian is too fast for me to catch, but all the girls laugh.

Flirting. He's flirting with them at my expense. A pang stabs me in the chest as an unexpected wave of tears burns my eyes.

*They're laughing at me.*

*I'm not pretty enough. Skinny enough.*

*Just...not enough.*

My hands tremble from the rejection, the skin on my face suddenly itchy, pulled too tightly across my cheek-bones. My heartbeat thumps in my ears, in my temples, blocking out the noise of the street so all I can hear is Lorenzo's growl.

Damn this man. Just fifteen minutes ago, I was breathing in this city like I never had oxygen before and now, now I want to suffocate.

My humiliation morphs into anger as I watch him retreat back into the restaurant. I'm supposed to be living my best life, embracing a new beginning. This is not the way I want my first day of my new life to start.

Standing from my table, my knees wobbly from a mixture of nerves, shame, and outrage, I exit the patio, ignoring the pitying look from Ms. Italy at table three.

Turning down a side street, I press my back against the old stone of an apartment building and close my eyes. Tears collect in the corners and I blink furiously to hold them at bay.

Ballerina Mia would sob.

Ballerina Mia would be crushed.

But I'm not Ballerina Mia anymore.

Taking a steadying breath, I continue my walk until another restaurant with a cute patio calls to me.

I sit and order an espresso.

I embrace the college pact.

———

"YAY! YOU'RE HERE!" The door to the Franchetti's apartment opens and I stumble forward. "I'm so sorry I wasn't home to meet you when you arrived. I thought your flight was later. Anyway, I'm Lexi, the other study abroad student staying here."

"Hi, I'm Mia."

"Come on in. Paola and Gianluca are still at work but they're meeting us for dinner tonight. You're going to adore them. They're super cool and young and love to travel. They just got back from a holiday in Spain – isn't that a song? Anyway, I saw that you put your suitcases in the room on the right; I hope you don't mind I took the room with two windows." She teeters on her toes, glancing at me.

"No, it's cool. I'm fine with any room."

"Good." She lets out a breath. "Are you tired?"

"Um, no, not really. I slept on the flight." I try to follow her random thoughts, tossing my purse on the bed.

"Perfect! I'll finish getting ready and let you settle in. We're supposed to meet Paola and Gianluca at the restaurant at 8:00PM but we can grab an aperitivo first, right? God, everything just sounds so much better, classier, in Italian, don't you think?"

"Uh, sure."

"The bathroom is right across the hall if you need to freshen up. Can you believe we have a bidet? My mother would die with how European it all is. I guess we can shave our legs in it."

Snorting, I laugh with Lexi. "You remind me of a hybrid of two of my friends, Emma and Lila."

"See, it's kismet that we were paired together. I'm so relieved to be paired with another student. This is going to be an amazing semester. I just know we're going to have the best time in Rome!" Lexi grabs my hand, giving my fingers a squeeze.

Taking in her hopeful expression, I commit to the pact all over again, letting my irritation and embarrassment from earlier fade away. Determined to have an epic senior year, I smile. "You're right."

"Yay!" Lexi squeals, hugging me. "Okay, go get ready. In thirty minutes, we'll be sipping wine."

Entering my room, I turn toward the mirror, scrunching the roots of my hair for volume. No go; my hair collapses back down, pin straight to below my shoulder blades. Meh. With my pale complexion and dark eyes, purple half-moons stamped beneath them, I look like an evil vampire.

Freshening up quickly and changing my clothes, I'm ready when Lexi knocks on my bedroom door.

───────

"Favorite city?" Lexi asks me over a glass of wine.

"New York. I'm from there."

"Oh really? I should have guessed. You totally have an East Coast vibe going on."

"Unapproachable?"

"No," she laughs, "just more serious. I'm from California, the Bay area."

"I've never been to the West Coast."

"Shut up! Are you serious? You'll have to come visit next semester."

Grinning at her invitation, I nod. Lexi is extra, but in a good way. Outside of dance, I've always done better in the shadows, away from the spotlight. That's why I click so well with Emma, Lila, and Maura. And now, Lexi.

"Favorite Hollywood crush?"

"What?" I choke on my wine, laughing.

"You know, like your Hollywood hall pass hookup?"

I shake my head.

"The famous guy your one-day husband will excuse you for cheating on him with."

"Oh my God. I don't know!"

"Mine's Zac Efron."

Rolling my eyes, I snort. "Good to know."

"Do you have a boyfriend?"

"I feel like we're speed dating for friends."

Lexi laughs. "Sorry, I don't mean to interrogate you."

I raise an eyebrow, taking another gulp of wine. Maura was right; this is nectar from the Gods.

"But, do you have a boyfriend?" she repeats.

"Nope. Do you?"

"Hell no! Who the hell would come to Rome with a man back home? I'm here for the food and the guys. Why'd you choose Rome?"

"It was one of my mom's dreams."

"Aw, that's so sweet! She must be so happy you're here." Lexi clutches my arm.

"She passed when I was nine."

"Oh shit. I'm sorry, Mia."

"No, it's okay. It's actually nice to talk about her sometimes. I found a bunch of her old journals and the one theme in all of them was travel, all the places she wanted to see. She was a free spirit, which is so funny, because it's the opposite of my dad. He's completely practical. Like me." I shrug, the wine already affecting me. Just rambling away. "Anyway, I wanted to come for her."

"That's really special."

"Yeah. Do you speak Italian?"

Lexi wrinkles her nose. "I can get by, kind of. Like I can order food and ask where the bathroom and the bar are."

"Important to know."

"Right? Oh, we're going to be late." She glances at her watch. "Ready to meet the Franchetti's?"

"Absolutely." I'm ready for whatever Rome throws my way.

---

I LIED.

One-hundred percent lying over here.

Liar liar pants on fire.

Because I am not ready for Angelina's.

Yet, that's where we are having dinner tonight.

As soon as Lexi points to Angelina's patio, my blood turns to ice and I falter on the cobblestone.

It has nothing to do with my one glass of wine. Honest.

"Ciao ragazze! We're here!" A petite woman, Paola, waves a hand in the air as we draw closer to the patio. She smiles, her dark hair cut short with a streak of blue slanting over her right eyebrow. How cool is she? Like an aspirational mama bear.

Gianluca grins next to her, a heavy five o'clock shadow covering his jaw. His arms are covered in tattoos, extending all the way to his fingers.

Who are these people? I thought host parents were supposed to be grandparent-y. But Paola and Gianluca are… #lifegoals.

"Benvenuti a Roma, Mia! We're so happy you're here." Paola welcomes me, kissing both of my cheeks and pulling me in for a hug, as if I'm her long-lost cousin and not the foreign exchange student she got stuck with for the semester.

I like her already.

"I swear I usually cook," Gianluca promises, placing his hand over his heart, as he pulls out my chair.

Lexi snorts but Paola shakes her head, "No, it's true. He usually does cook. I'm better at this." She holds up her full wine glass.

I force a smile, sitting down, my eyes darting from Paola to Gianluca to the restaurant, searching for some sign of *him*.

Gianluca, good man, fills mine and Lexi's wine glasses. If I was ever going to really take up drinking, now would be a perfect time to start.

"Salute." He raises his wine and we all clink our glasses. I take two large gulps, the wine heating me up with courage and…gumption.

"Wait until you girls see the waiter. He is divine." Paola whispers, earning a look from Gianluca. She blows him a kiss and he shakes his head.

Lexi grins at their adorableness while my stomach sinks to my toes and keeps on going, right to the Earth's core, where the temperature is 10,800 degrees Fahrenheit. That's nearly 1,000 degrees hotter than the sun's surface and right now, I rival the sun as my insides burn up with a heady cocktail of nerves, anger, and embarrassment.

"Don't go corrupting these young women, Paola. They are here to study, to learn the language, experience the culture…"

While I nod along with Gianluca's summary of our program, Lexi snorts.

"Oh, please. I'm here to have a fantastic story about falling in lust and gaining a million pounds." Lexi interjects. "And this one already speaks Italian." She swats my arm.

Gianluca rolls his eyes as Paola grins.

"Wait until you see the waiter." She repeats, leaning forward. "He's a professional race car driver and his name is —"

"Another bottle of red wine," our waiter announces, placing a second bottle of the house wine on our table with a flourish.

Glancing up from underneath my eyelashes, my humiliation skyrockets. It's him. Of course it is.

When has God ever loved me?

Because I'm staring at him, I see the moment he recognizes me. His eyes, the most serene shade of blue, widen and he inhales sharply.

Scraping a palm along his jaw, his eyes bore into mine. "Ciao." His voice is nearly a whisper, dancing down my spine on a wave of nerves.

Blinking, I glance at my menu, relieved when Gianluca asks Lorenzo about the specials. The table orders and too soon his gaze lingers on me.

"And for you?" His blue eyes slam into mine and I pinch my leg under the table to center myself. *I will not let this man fluster me. I will not be flustered. I am unflappable.*

*And tipsy.*

"The caprese salad, please." I order in Italian, proud when my voice doesn't waver.

"Perfetto." He says, as if he's trying to compliment me. Too little, too late, I look away as he repeats our order.

"Si." Paola gathers the menus and hands them to him.

"Okay, grazie." He lingers a beat too long, his gaze studying my profile as I refuse to turn my head.

The tiniest puff of breath escapes his lips before he retreats back to the restaurant.

"Relax girl, he's only the first Italian we've met, except for these two." Lexi nods toward Paola and Gianluca.

Great, she thinks I have some weird crush on Lorenzo. I suppose it's better than the alternative, the truth. That he finds me lacking in every way imaginable.

Paola waves a hand. "Don't worry. He's used to it; women fall at Lorenzo's feet. Trust me, he likes the attention."

"Lorenzo." Lexi repeats. "Super sexy name." She flips her hair over her shoulder.

Gianluca snorts, "The three of you girls together is going to be trouble."

"Nah, it's men like that who are the trouble." Lexi points to where Lorenzo slipped back into the restaurant.

I finish my wine.

Gianluca grins. "I think he likes our Mia."

"Oh no." I shake my head. "He definitely doesn't like me.

Besides, I don't know how to do this." I gesture toward the space Lorenzo vacated.

"Flirt?" Paola asks, refilling my glass.

"Life?" Lexi guesses and I stick my tongue out at her.

She chuckles. "Trust me, Mia. I know when a hottie is into a body, and that man is into yours. Oh my God, why are you turning red?"

"I'm starting to dislike you."

"Pssh, impossible. Everyone likes me."

"See, you're already bickering like sisters." Gianluca sips his wine, tossing an arm around Paola's shoulders. "You make us so proud."

"I'm going to hook you up with Lorenzo." Lexi decides, her face serious.

"No way!" I protest, reaching out to grab her forearm.

"I'll help." Paola volunteers.

"You guys, I'm not cut out for this. I don't do flirting and dates, I don't — that stupid pact, I —"

"What pact?" Gianluca asks.

"That's your takeaway? Really?" I ask him and he laughs.

"Tell us about the pact, cara." He rubs his hands together, hunching over the table. "Just so you know, you two are already the most interesting foreign exchange students we've had."

"And the best." Paola adds sweetly.

"You've known me for thirty minutes." I point out, picking up my wine again.

"Well they've known me for twenty-four hours; I'm carrying your weight at the moment." Lexi snorts.

Glancing down at my fleshy thighs, I bite my tongue to keep the swell of emotions at bay. I know it's an expression and Lexi isn't referring to my literal body weight. But if she was, she wouldn't be able to carry me. Not anymore.

"Mia, I'm kidding, I —"

"It's fine. I made a college pact with my best friends before I flew out." I say, explaining the pact to the table.

"Oh, now I am definitely hooking you up!" Lexi exclaims when I'm finished.

"Cara," Gianluca says, "you're in Roma now. Embrace this pact of yours. You're supposed to fall in love here. It's the city of love."

"Isn't that Paris?" I ask.

"Yeah, I thought Rome was the Eternal City." Lexi scrunches her eyebrows.

"Well done, girls. For that, more wine!" Paola lifts her wine glass.

Shaking my head, I stand. "Excuse me. I'm going to find the bathroom."

"Inside to your left." Paola offers.

Standing, my head buzzes from the wine and I grip the underside of the table. Shaking it off, I slip inside the restaurant and locate the bathroom down a hallway off the main dining area.

After washing my hands, I study my reflection in the mirror. My cheeks are flushed and my eyes bright from the wine. Taking a fortifying breath, I pull open the door, step into the hallways, and collide with —

"Lorenzo." I gasp as his hands encircle my waist, steadying me.

He tilts his head, his gaze sweeping over my face, his eyes darkening.

"Excuse me." I clear my throat, stepping out of his hold.

"Why'd you leave before?"

"What?"

"Earlier today. Why'd you leave?" His eyes flash, dropping to my lips, and back up again.

Humiliation rolls through me, drowning all logical thought until I'm left with shame and anger. "Why do you think?"

He smirks. "Because I wasn't paying enough attention to you?"

"Wow, you really think highly of yourself."

He chuckles, bracing his forearm against the wall, leaning closer to me. "Then why'd you leave?"

"Something came up." I cling to my wine-induced bravery with both hands. *I am unflappable!*

"Like what?"

"That's none of your business." I fold my arms across my chest, snorting when his eyes dip to my lips. *Now he's interested?*

"What's your name?"

"Also none of your business."

"Are you always this unreasonable?"

I swallow, his word choice striking a chord. Because I'm the most reasonable person I know. I'm the ultimate people pleaser, a yes girl. But this man, Lorenzo, scrapes at my feelings with one dismissive retort, causing my blood to simmer and my chest to ache.

Dipping my head, I start to step around him. "Excuse me."

"Wait." His hand snakes out, gripping my upper arm, stopping me. His eyes scan mine, his expression slipping. "Are you going to cry?"

Blink. Blink. Blink.

*Why is this my life? Why is this happening?*

"Look, I thought we were joking around. It's not a big deal that you split this afternoon. I mean, you hadn't even ordered." He frowns, the lines on either side of his mouth deepening.

I shake off his hand and step toward the patio.

I'm nearly to the door when he whispers, "What's your name, bellezza?"

*Beauty.*

*Why did he have to go and call me beauty?*

"Mia."

# 3

## LORENZO

S he's different.

The two girls eating on the patio with Gianluca and Paola are both beautiful but it's the brunette who draws my attention. At first glance, there's nothing remarkable about her. In fact, when she sat down at Angelina's earlier today, I was annoyed.

Mama had just spewed some bullshit about me upholding our family legacy.

Giulietta was flashing more skin than usual, enticing me to make her my hook-up for tonight.

And the brunette sat down and ogled me like she's never talked to a man before.

I didn't have the time, or patience, for her sweet, innocent routine. Because no girls studying in Roma for a semester are *that* innocent. Still, when I came back to take her order and she was gone, guilt rocked through me.

I was a dick.

And for no reason at all.

Mama would have been supremely disappointed.

And Papa would have rolled over in his grave.

My eyes cut to her again. Mia.

A quiet intensity flows through her, a hidden strength. Sure, she oozes sweetness and sincerity but her eyes, dark like chocolate, are perceptive, intelligent. In a world filled with glitter facades and imitations, this girl is the real deal; she's alluring because she is unaware of her appeal.

While other women flaunt themselves, dressing provocatively, laughing too loud, she sits quietly, her dark eyes observing, her lips tipping up at the corners, as if she's concealing a secret. Like the Mona freaking Lisa.

The blonde laughs again, several men on the street turning in her direction. American girls are always an entertaining distraction. But Mia, she's more than that; she's a puzzling mystery.

Shaking myself out of this pointless examination, I approach her table.

"All finished?" I ask as Gianluca slips me his card.

"Si, tutto era delizioso. Grazie."

*Everything was delicious.* Eyeing Mia's full plate, I'm not so sure. *Maybe she's nervous? Homesick?*

*Or maybe I affect her.*

The thought causes a thrill to tug at my abdomen which is stupid; I shouldn't make a woman so nervous she can't eat.

"These are our new foreign exchange students, Lexi and Mia." Paola introduces the girls. "They'll be staying with us the next four months. Keep an eye on them; your mama says you'll be spending a lot of time at Angelina's and I'm sure they'll be here studying with their friends."

"Certo." *Of course.* "Here are some sweets for later." I pass Lexi a paper bag.

Peeking into the bag, she groans. "So yummy. They're biscotti." She says to her beguiling friend.

Mia nods, her cheeks stained pink, her eyes avoiding mine. "Grazie."

"So, Lorenzo, what are the best clubs to hit up?" Lexi asks.

"You could have asked me." Gianluca interjects.

Lexi snorts as Paola laughs.

Grinning, I rattle off a few places the American students like to visit.

Gianluca frowns, "Tell them a few local spots too."

"Va bene. There's Ghiaccio, but it's more of a bar, and —"

"Wait, I'm not going to remember all these. Let me just grab your number so…" She peers into her purse, frowning. "Damn, I left my phone at home. Mia," she turns to her friend, "give Lorenzo your phone so we can message him later about the clubs."

Mia's eyes widen, a flicker of panic edging her irises, vulnerability glittering in their depths. Then she blinks, checking the emotion. Instead, her gaze darts between Lexi and me.

Smirking, I hold out a hand, knowing she doesn't want my number. And for some reason, that makes me want to give it to her so much more than if she begged me for it.

"Bellezza?" I prompt, noting how Gianluca freezes and Lexi's eyes widen.

Mia rolls her eyes, huffing, as she reaches into her purse and extracts her phone. When she passes it to me, our hands touch, the warmth of her skin pressing into mine. Glancing at her, her chocolate eyes are fathomless, dark and deep and overflowing with so much emotion.

I punch in my contact information. Right before I hand back her phone, I call myself so I'll have her number too. "If you need anything while you're here, call me." I bend my knees until I catch Mia's eyes so she knows I'm serious.

She nods, the corner of her mouth lifting into the tiniest smile.

At the sight of her smile, some of the tightness in my chest eases and I grin back, relieved that this girl doesn't think the worst of me, which is ridiculous because why the hell do I care?

"Don't hit on my kid, Enzo." Gianluca jokes.

Mia blushes, snorting as I clap Gianluca on the shoulders. "You're showing your age."

"For that, I'm taking back your tip."

"Please. Everyone knows Europeans don't tip."

"That's the truth." Lexi comments.

"Go help your mama." Gianluca flips his chin toward the restaurant.

"Ciao."

"Ciao." The Franchetti's and their study abroad charges exit the patio.

Watching Mia leave, something shifts in my chest. Staring at her petite form, the soft sway of her hips, I groan. *What the fuck is wrong with me?* She's just some girl who ate at Angelina's. A college kid living with the Franchetti's for the semester. She means nothing.

And yet, even I know that is a lie.

Because I'm already thinking about messages to send her when I usually would delete her number.

"Table four wants dessert," Simona whispers, her breath tickling my cheek. She leans closer, pressing her breasts against my back as she grabs the wine bottle and empty glasses from the table.

"Right." I turn back to the restaurant, ignoring Simona's

advances, my thoughts preoccupied by the puzzling brunette with soulful eyes who didn't eat dinner.

---

FLIPPING the lock to Angelina's, I grip the back of my neck, massaging it. I'm exhausted and not used to being on my feet for so many consecutive hours. As much as I want to go home and drop into a coma, I agreed to meet Sandro for a few drinks.

*Sandro: Are you coming?*

*Me: On my way.*

Driving to the bar, I scan the students littering the streets, falling out of bars, posing for selfies. It's ridiculous, but I'm looking for her. *Mia.* Is she one of the girls laughing amidst a group of friends, updating her Instagram account, taking shots of limoncello? I doubt it. She doesn't strike me as the party girl type.

Still, a lot of these American study abroad students cut loose the semester they visit Europe. For many of them, they can't legally drink in America. In Rome, they can do it all — drink, party, and travel, all on their parents' credit card. Who wouldn't take advantage of that opportunity? I should have studied abroad when I was in university; I would have gone to New York.

After trolling for two blocks with no sign of Mia, I hang a left and park the car. Sidestepping an American kid already puking on the sidewalk, I pull open the door to Ghiaccio, a bar Sandro and I frequent.

Spotting Sandro, I walk over to him and the two beautiful women he's chatting up at the bar, a drink dangling from his left hand. Serious, composed, his expression flat, getting

Sandro to crack a smile is as easy as keeping the seat clean while pissing drunk.

"Ciao Enzo." Sandro greets me. "Meet Aileen and Kerry." He motions toward the two girls sitting at the bar. "They're visiting Rome. From Ireland." His eyebrows bend as I easily read his thoughts. *Want to bang a couple of Irish girls?*

The left side of my mouth tugs up in acquiescence and I accept the Negroni from the bartender. Facing the girls, I turn on my natural charm. This type of exchange is routine for Sandro and me; we play our roles well. Sandro is the moody, unavailable but mysterious stranger. I'm the engaging and arrogant best friend.

I lift my Negroni, "To a beautiful night with new friends."

They giggle, as expected. I wink, as required. Sandro drinks, as usual.

An hour later, I bang Ailene and he takes Kerry.

# SEPTEMBER

# 4

## MIA

L orenzo: *Good luck tomorrow.*
    *Me: Hey…???*
*Lorenzo: First day of class.*
*Me: Why are you messaging me?*
*Lorenzo: Because you didn't message me.*
*Me: I don't need any help.*
*Lorenzo: Sure about that?*
*Me: What's that supposed to mean?*
*Lorenzo: Come to Angelina's tomorrow.*

Gah! This man is infuriating. I have no idea what he's talking about half the time; it's as if we are having two completely different conversations.

And why is he messaging me? After all the awkwardness between us, why would he want me to pass by Angelina's? What's his game?

Up late thinking all the thoughts about Lorenzo, a guy who is probably out with another woman as I analyze his text message punctuation, messes with my head.

I can't sleep.

At all.

Sure, it's partly nerves.

But the other part is…

Far, far worse.

All I can think about is how many calories I consumed this weekend.

Carbohydrates.

Sugar.

Gelato, just so I could snap a photo of myself pretending to eat it in front of the Trevi Fountain and send it to the girls.

*Cornetto. Salad. Yogurt. Piece of bread. Pasta e fagioli soup.*

It's an endless loop in my mind, reminding me how disgusting I am. My stomach grumbles and I squeeze my eyes closed, wishing I didn't feel like this. Wishing I didn't think these thoughts.

After an hour of restless tossing and turning, I escape to the bathroom. Leaving the light off so I don't have to see my reflection in the mirror, I squat in front of the toilet.

Screwing my eyes closed, I visualize my full cheeks, my double chin, and flabby thighs. It's not difficult, my imperfections flood my mind like a tsunami.

In the handful of months since I lost ballet, my ballerina body as morphed into a linebacker.

And as much as I want to shed aspects of Ballerina Mia, I don't want to look like this. Feel like this.

Disgusting.

Weighed down.

Obese.

Pulling my hair into a messy bun, I flip up the toilet seat. Then, I press two fingers to the back of my throat and heave.

Again.

The contents of my stomach spill into the toilet.

Again.

Liquid gushes down my chin and dribbles onto the toilet seat.

*Get it together, Mia.*

Again.

Once my throat burns, raw, my mind settles. Relief courses through me; I feel lighter, cleaner.

Refreshed.

Brushing my teeth, I enjoy the sting in my mouth, the pain a reminder of my purity.

Emptiness is its own type of delicious.

---

*A rain of flowers descended*
  *(sweet in the memory)*
  *from the beautiful branches into her lap,*
  *and she sat there*
  *humble amongst such glory,*
  *covered now by the loving shower.*
  *A flower fell on her hem,*
  *one in her braided blonde hair,*
  *that was seen on that day to be*
  *like chased gold and pearl:*
  *one rested on the ground, and one in the water,*
  *and one, in wandering vagary,*
  *twirling, seemed to say: 'Here Love rules'.*
  *-Petrarch, Il Canzoniere Sonnet 126*

AFTER AN HOUR LECTURE of Italian Literature on Monday, Professoressa dismisses us with a clap of her hands. "Don't forget to introduce yourselves and make some friends. You will all be working closely together this semester."

"Hey," the guy sitting next to me leans over. "I'm Peter Buchanan. Call me Pete."

"Mia."

"Nice to meet you." He shoves a notebook into his backpack, glancing at me. With sandy hair, a lopsided grin, and dressed in a Polo shirt with khakis, Pete reminds me of most of the guys from McShain University.

"You too."

"Ready for this class?"

"I hope so. I've always wanted to read Italian classics — like Dante — in Italian."

"Yeah, well, I'm pretty nervous. I don't think I understand them that well in English." He laughs.

Smiling back, I nod.

He stalls, biting his bottom lip. "Any chance you want to exchange numbers and study sometime?"

"Oh, yeah, sure."

"Great. Let me give you my number then." He reaches over and scribbles his number into the corner of my notebook. "Maybe we can get together after class next week?"

"Yeah. Perfect."

"Okay. See ya around, Mia."

Pete shuffles out of the classroom after Professoressa. Looking around, I'm the only person still seated. And I am stunned.

No one ever asks me to work on anything. At McShain, I was labeled as a control freak and most of my classmates avoided me like the plague when it came to group projects of study sessions.

To be fair, they were mostly right.

But this is a fresh start. A new beginning.

Somehow, I snagged the numbers of two hot guys in one week!

AFTER A SUCCESSFUL FIRST class of *Italian Literature*, I debate whether or not I should stop by Angelina's like Lorenzo suggested.

What's the point? It's not like he likes me…

Except, sheer curiosity wins my internal debate and I walk to the restaurant, a giddiness riding low in my belly. As much as I want to pretend I'm unaffected by Lorenzo, it's a big, fat, lie. Because he's already under my skin.

The only man who has ever made me react so brazenly.

The only guy who has flirted with me by insulting me.

The only one who has me curious enough to subject myself to more insults.

There is a gentle breeze and it feels nice to sit on the patio, the sunshine warming my skin. Pulling out my copy of Dante's *Il Inferno*, a notebook, and the course syllabus, I place them on the table and flip through the menu. Might as well start studying while I'm here.

"Bellezza, you're here." Lorenzo saunters over. Blocking out the sun, it shines around him, brightening parts of his face, shadowing others, like a Caravaggio painting.

Striking, authoritative, larger than life, his presence alone swallows the air around us and I find myself lightheaded from his lingering glance.

He's unlike any of my male friends — all dancers or drama students.

There isn't anything artsy about him. He doesn't float when he walks, he swaggers, his body exuding a different type of confidence. Each step is with purpose, intent. Even in an apron he emits masculinity and machismo.

The longer I stare, the more his smile spreads, until his

dimples appear, and I wonder what it would be like to trace them with my finger.

"I heard Angelina's is a great place to study." I finally answer.

He chuckles, winking. It's seductive yet familiar, aloof but intimate. "What can I get for you?"

"The artichoke and roasted pepper salad please. And a water." I close the menu.

"*Il Inferno*?" he fingers my book.

"Yes. Have you read it?"

"*In that book which is my memory,*
    *On the first page of the chapter that is the day when I*
*first met you,*
    *Appear the words, 'Here begins a new life,'*"
    -Dante Alighieri, *La Vita Nuova*

"I'll be right back with your water."

As soon as he is back in the restaurant, I thumb through my paperback copy of *Il Inferno* looking for the quote.

Lorenzo sets down a water glass moments later. "You won't find it in there."

I glance up, my finger bookmarking my page. "What do you mean? I thought it was Dante."

"It is." He slips into the chair across from me, pulling the book from my hand and losing my page. "It's from an earlier work, *La Vita Nuova*. You should read that first. It's beautiful; a collection of poetry, all love and romance, for his muse Beatrice."

"And you've read it?" I can't keep the edge of sarcasm from my voice as I study him. He seems sincere, but the dimple winking from his cheek makes me feel like he's teasing me.

"I've read all the classics."

I narrow my eyes.

"You know, '*books have led some to learning and others to madness.*'"

"That's not Dante." I say, even though I'm not sure.

"It's not."

"Who?" I dip my head toward him.

He traps his bottom lip between his teeth, his eyes flickering with an emotion I can't place but it causes an awareness to hum through my body. The air between us crackles with energy, heavy like the air before a summer rainstorm.

Reaching over, his finger trails along the table until the blunt edge taps my syllabus. "Petrarca," he pronounces the poet's name in Italian, his voice huskier then it was moments ago.

"Petrarch said that? Are you sure? Doesn't he only write about love?" I ramble, nerves zinging through my body.

Lorenzo blinks, shaking his head slowly, a grin spreading across his mouth. He sighs, leaning closer. "Bellezza, if that's what you think, then I really better leave you alone to study."

I blush and he tilts his head, misinterpreting the color flooding my cheeks.

"Or, I could help you." His fingers wrap around mine on top of the table, squeezing with the slightest pressure, like a promise. "Next time, message me, Mia."

"We'll see, Lorenzo."

"Call me Enzo." His fingertips slide over the delicate skin on the inside of my wrist.

"Enzo." I repeat, breathless, distracted by his touch.

He smirks, his gaze holding mine. The heat that flickers in his eyes intensifies, flaring into a hunger, a desire so sharp I feel it in my toes. Desperate to look away but unable to drag my eyes from his, I stare back, watch as the flames combust, into raw need.

Holy cannoli. My breath traps in my lungs, my body almost trembling from Lorenzo's gaze.

The moment stretches between us, a tension so palpable I can taste it, before Lorenzo's eyelids dip and he clears his throat.

His fingers dig into the soft flesh of my wrist as he leans closer. Every move he makes is deliberate, with intent, and this is no different.

Captivated, I can barely breathe, never mind blink.

"The readings by Boccaccio will entertain you. The readings by Dante will cause you to question, to think. But Petrarca," he shakes his head, "you will fall in love with his words, with his unyielding passion for Laura. Such a love, it's nothing to be mocked or laughed at but celebrated and yearned for. Every woman deserves to be a muse once in her life, no?" his breath fans across my skin, my eyes dropping to his lip, entranced, enamored, completely enchanted.

I nod slowly. Gathering my wits, I manage to quote back, "'*To be able to say how much you love is to love but little.*'"

Lorenzo stills, his fingers hovering above the pulse of my wrist, his eyes searing into mine. He blinks, breaking the moment. "Petrarca. Where did you learn that?"

"In my mother's journal."

"And did you get caught reading her journal?" he whispers, dropping my wrist and settling back in his chair.

"No. My mom passed away when I was nine."

A shadow falls over his face as he averts his gaze. "Excuse me for joking around."

This time, I'm the one reaching out, placing a tentative hand on his forearm. His skin is hot against my palm, corded with muscle. He doesn't pull away and I stare at where my hand touches him, noting how pale my skin is against his olive tones. "It's okay. Really. I like talking about her."

"My papa passed about six months back. Pulmonary fibrosis." He rubs a hand over his forehead, shielding his eyes from view.

"Oh, Lorenzo, I'm so sorry."

"No, it's okay. You are right. Sometimes it is nice to talk about him, to still have him as part of my day, a part of my life."

I nod, understanding his desire to share details about his father but at the same time, keep them all for himself. "Was this his restaurant?"

He turns, his gaze drinking in Angelina's Ristorante. "No, this was my great-grandfather's restaurant. He started it in 1907. Then it passed to my grandfather who didn't have any sons. So now, it belongs to Mama." He smirks at me. "And she loves this place. Since my papa's passing, it's become a sanctuary for her."

"Is that why you work here?"

"You know, I'm not exactly sure why I'm working here."

"I thought you were a race car driver."

His lips tick up at the corners. "Asking around about me?"

"Hardly. You do know Paola and Gianluca, right?"

"Ah, Paola told you."

I nod. "Why'd you stop?"

A shadow shifts across his face, like a cloud snuffing out the sun, all his brightness turns grey. "That's a story for another day." He flips his chin toward a couple approaching the patio. Lorenzo stands and indicates that he will be with them in a moment. "You carried our entire conversation in Italian. You'll be fluent before you leave Rome, more so if you message me." He raises his eyebrows, his dimple flashing.

"Why are you being so nice to me now?" I blurt out, blushing as soon as the words are in the air between us.

Lorenzo studies me for a long moment, an emotion I can't read washing over his features. "You're unexpected."

*Oh jeez, what does that mean?*

"In a good way." He adds.

"I'd rather call you Lorenzo."

He stares at me for a long moment before turning to greet the couple.

# 5

## LORENZO

My eyes close as Francesca bobs her mouth up and down, up and down, over my dick. I run my fingers through her hair, clenching it tightly in my fists. Should have done this months ago. But Sandro was still banging her in July and it seemed best to wait a few weeks, make sure he didn't catch anything before I messed around with her.

Not that I'll fuck her. I've never been into sloppy seconds, but if she wants to swing by to get me off, who am I to stop her? She groans loudly, her palms gliding up my thighs, her right hand fisting in the hem of my T-shirt. She moans again.

*Stop with the show and just suck, sweetheart.*

Francesca's downright slamming, even though she's nearing thirty. Too bad she's saddled with a reputation; despite her many talents, no one in my circle takes her seriously. Too much drama, too much baggage, too many stories.

The one thing working in her favor today is that she's a brunette, which beckons a flood of unintended thoughts about another brunette.

The one invading my mind.

Mia.

She came to Angelina's every day this week for lunch, a natural Beatrice without a clue. She could easily inspire the works of an incredible poet, artist, creative without realizing it. Incredibly sweet, with a vulnerability shining around her like a halo, she also possesses this burning curiosity. An untapped passion that skirts the edges of all of our interactions. It's just on the cusp of lighting her up if she'll let it.

Each day, I watch her murmur the words from Dante's Canti, her eyes flaring with intensity, her hand scribbling notes. She calls to me like one of Homer's Sirens. All of these heightened senses and overwhelming feelings toward a woman I've never even kissed.

I'm about to fucking shipwreck myself.

Glancing at the top of Francesca's head, I grip her hair harder, encouraging her to move faster. Ah, that's it. Closing my eyes, I block her out and pretend she's Mia. That the noises falling from her lips are the sounds Mia would make. That the hair knotting around my knuckles belongs to sweet Mia.

And I come.

Hard and fast.

Mia's name on my lips.

---

*JAB, jab, one-two, hook. Jab, jab, one-two, hook.*

My gloves pound against the pads Sandro holds. Muscles in my shoulders and arms burn, and I welcome the sting; it's been too long since I've hit the gym.

"Pick up the pace," Sandro comments as I throw a left jab.

I focus on the pads, weaving as he comes at me.

*Come on, Enzo. Keep your elbows in. Gloves up. Don't drop your hands.*

Sandro swipes at me again, and I step back, faltering. I swear and a rare smile cracks his face as he tries to knock me back farther. Throwing a four-punch combo, some of the excessive energy running through my veins leaks out.

Fifteen minutes later, sweat pours down my spine, the fabric of my T-shirt sticking to me.

"What's with you today?" Sandro wipes a towel against the back of his neck.

"What do you mean?"

"You seem like you're on edge. All straight?"

"Yeah. Just, been busy. I need a night out."

I have too much on my mind. There's fudged ledgers, issues with the vineyards, not to mention all the hours I've been logging at Angelina's. Claudia's mention of Zio Benito hangs over my head like a dark cloud. And, I'm spending too many nights drinking, trying to fuck a beautiful brunette out of my system, even though I haven't had one taste of her sweet mouth.

I desperately need to blow off steam and since I'm keeping my head down, not seeking out any digs or races, my options are limited.

"Want to hit the club tonight?" Sandro asks, taking a swig from his water bottle.

Blowing out a breath, I nod slowly. It's not a bad idea; I haven't been to the club in a long time and rolling with our usual crew promises to be both distracting and entertaining.

"Sure. I'll meet you there."

And I'll try not to go home with a random brunette.

# 6

# MIA

"Oh, I like," Lexi comments, holding up a pale shimmery eye shadow I bought this week.

"Thanks." I close my eyes as Lexi walks over to me, the eye shadow clasped in her hand and the brush already poised to swipe across my eyelid. As she works her magic, the beat bumping out of the travel speakers she hooked up to her laptop changes. "I love this song."

"Total throwback." Lexi agrees. "Sexy and sultry or sweet and playful?"

"What?"

"What look are you going for tonight?"

"Lexi, the only time I've ever really worn makeup, was for onstage performances."

"Oh." She grimaces. "That's scary."

Snorting, I nod. "So please, work your magic."

"On it." She's quiet for the next few minutes, her brows dipping together in concentration. "Okay. You're done."

Turning toward the mirror, I gasp. I look…pretty. Like, Lila-worthy prettiness. The type of beauty that causes men to look twice and women to stare harder. My eyes glimmer, bright and bold, my cheekbones appear higher, my lips fuller. "Lexi, thank you." I whisper, ignoring the emotion swelling in my chest that could turn into tears if I don't shut it down.

I'm really doing this, reinventing myself. Snapping a selfie, I message it to the girls.

*Me: #CollegePactLife*

"Stop. You know you're a skinny bitch." she dances over to my desk where our second bottle of wine sits. Popping out the cork, she pours two glasses and hands one to me. "To dancing our asses off."

"You look insanely hot," I sip my wine, checking out her deep red, short dress with a plunging neckline.

She bows, walking over to her makeup bag to dig out a body shimmer. I snort as she brushes shimmer across her breasts. "What's that for?"

"So the guys focus right where I want 'em to," she explains.

I roll my eyes. Only Lexi. And maybe Lila.

"Put this on." Lexi hands me a very tiny, very short, very sexy green dress.

"I don't know, I —"

"Think of your pact." She reminds me, tilting her head. "I have the perfect earrings." She turns, rummaging through a drawer before holding up a pair of chandelier earrings.

I wait until her attention is focused on a stack of gold bangle bracelets before I undress and slip into the green dress.

"You look hot as fuck," Lexi comments when she turns around. "I wish I was as skinny as you."

"I'm not."

"Gah! Don't be one of those girls. Flaunt it." She points at my red toes. "I have wedges for that dress. What size do you wear?"

"Seven."

"Yay! Me too!" Lexi roots around in her closet. "Found them." She announces, handing me ridiculously high wedges. "We have to do wedges here, our stilettos will get stuck in the cobblestones. That's the only practical advice I got from my sorority regarding my study abroad."

"Makes sense." Slipping them on, I turn toward the full-length mirror. Woah. Lexi was right. This dress does make me look good. "Thanks Lexi. I think I'm ready."

"Hell yeah you are!"

<hr>

THE CLUB LEXI takes me to is private and exclusive and unlike any place I've ever been before.

The music is pulsing, the swarm of bodies on the dance floor moving in rhythm to the beat. Scantily clad servers with long legs and bare torsos weave in between the dancers, chatting with the men sitting at the cocktail tables, taking orders and delivering drinks. Occasionally, one of the cocktail servers tinkers a laugh as a well-dressed man, in a well-tailored jacket, slips folded up euros into her hand. Or the waistband of her shorts.

How do these women stay so thin, so tiny, when the unforgiving carbohydrates of pasta, pizza, and bread constantly surround them?

"What are you drinking?" Lexi shouts over the music.

"Whatever you're having."

Lexi orders us two prosecco-based drinks and two shots. "Tonight, we're celebrating!"

"What are we celebrating?"

"La vita Italiana!" she exclaims, turning to hand me a shot glass and sliding her credit card across the bar to start a tab.

"Thank you, Lexi!" I raise my shot.

"To an awesome semester with an amazing roomie."

Rolling my eyes, I clink glasses with her before tossing the alcohol back. Within seconds, my eyes tear and I choke around the burn in my throat. "What was that?"

"Tequila."

Oh shit. Lila and Emma drink tequila. Then they don't move from the couch for the rest of the weekend.

"Relax. I won't let anything happen to you. Live a little!" Lexi yells in my ear, handing me a champagne flute and taking a sip of hers.

I'm doing this, pushing past my comfort zone, embracing this adventure. Maura's words come back to me. *I'm being brave.*

Turning to the bartender, I order two more shots, handing over a twenty-euro note.

Lexi whoops in approval.

The alcohol hits me hard and before I know it, Lexi and I are dancing amidst a sea of bodies. Our arms wave above our heads, our hips swirl to the beat, our faces sport goofy grins and smeared eye shadow. And for once, I live a real college experience.

When a hard body steps up behind me, placing rough hands on my hips, pulling my frame back to grind against him, I don't fight it. I can tell from Lexi's expression that he's hot, so I close my eyes and enjoy it.

My skin feels sticky, too hot, as Lexi's dress clings to my frame. Pushing my hair out of my eyes, the guy's hands glide up my body, clasping my fingers in his and turning me around to face him. Catching a brief glimpse of his face assures me he's a tall, dark, and handsome. He offers a seductive smirk before his mouth descends on mine.

A thrill runs through me, bolstering my confidence.

But at the last moment, I duck out of his kiss.

Lexi swoops in to save me, our laughter mingling, as she drags me back to the bar.

Ordering two more flutes of prosecco, Lexi chats up the man next to her.

Resting my back against the bar, I drink in the scene. Beautiful women dance before me, their designer dresses riding up their skinny, tanned thighs. Tall, dark, and hand-somes touch the girls' hips invitingly and pull them closer as the music beats on. It's like a scene from a movie, one where everyone is ridiculously gorgeous, stupidly tanned, and perfectly thin.

Scanning the club, I note the roped-off VIP booths. There, guys pop champagne bottles and girls squeal as champagne showers erupt, droplets glistening in their hair. Squinting, my stomach drops to my toes, leaving a trail of emptiness in its wake. My skin itches, too hot, too sweaty as my chest tightens and my heart gallops.

Lorenzo.

Leaning over the railing of an exclusive area, a Negroni casually resting between his fingers, he is the epitome of every man my father warned me away from. Detached, indif-ferent, and so sexy he could be an advertising campaign in Times Square, my eyes drink him in like I'm dying of thirst. He's wearing a white dress shirt, rolled up on his forearms, dark hair dusting his tanned skin. His hair curls up around his collar, and he brushes a stray piece back from his forehead. Tapping a navy leather loafer in beat with the music, he smiles adoringly at the beautiful redhead beside him. His left dimple flashes as he leans closer to the woman and her green eyes shine like emeralds.

She throws her head back and laughs at whatever Lorenzo whispers in her ear. For some reason, it's as if I can hear it, even over the thumping bass and noise of the club. The sound is grating, like nails on a chalkboard, even though I know it's only in my head.

But I despise seeing Lorenzo with this flawless woman.

Because I'll never be pure sophistication and class like her.

And because a part of me, a stupid, naïve part of me, thought that maybe, Lorenzo could like me. Might look at me the way he's gazing at her.

Gah! It's like a train wreck.

I desperately need to look away and yet, I stare, entranced by their interaction. She places a hand on his shoulder and leans into his side, running her nose against his jawline, murmuring in his ear.

Amusement flits across his face before he turns, pulling her into his arms and disappearing into the throng of bodies in his VIP booth.

And I can't tear my eyes away.

Even though my stomach feels hollow, even though tears sting the back of my nose, even though I wish I never saw him in the first place.

An unfamiliar sensation that feels like fire spreads through my stomach, my face heating.

*Why am I upset about this?*

*I barely know him.*

*It's not like there was ever anything between us, right?*

*Lies. All of it lies.*

Because even though I shouldn't, a part of me feels betrayed.

Turning back to Lexi, I nudge her with my elbow. Not missing a beat, she says, "Mia, this is Pietro. Pietro, this is my friend Mia."

Pietro fits Lila's description of tall, dark, and handsome. Don't all the Italians seem to fulfill that criteria?

"Hi." I shake Pietro's hand.

"Nice to meet you." He tips his head toward his friend who steps into our circle. "This is Pepe."

"A pleasure," Pepe clasps my hand, rubbing his thumb over my knuckles. "Would you girls care for a drink?" He eyes Lexi's empty flute.

"Sure." She agrees.

Moments later, Pepe presses a shot glass into my hand. "Salute."

"Salute," the three of us echo and toss back our shots. The straight vodka burns for a moment and then warms my chest and belly, easing the jealousy eating at my stomach like acid.

Pietro hands me another drink.

Reality check.

I'm at a bar in Rome, chatting with two gorgeous men with delicious accents.

*Forget Lorenzo.*

*Live the pact, Mia.*

"Cheers."

---

I FORGOT how it feels to just enjoy dancing.

Without having to be the perfect ballerina.

Without the impossible standards and hopeless expectations.

At this club in Rome, right now, I embrace the pact. I give myself up to the moment, to the cadence of bodies swirling around me, and to the crisp taste of too many glasses of Prosecco.

As my body loosens up, I enjoy the music, the beat, the rhythm. I enjoy dancing.

Sliding my hands up Pepe's arms, I clasp my fingers

behind his broad shoulders and step closer. My hips automatically sync to the beat, and I close my eyes, enjoying the feel of his chest against mine.

"Woo! Get it girl!" Lexi calls out behind me.

As the song fades into the next beat, I open my eyes and snort at the circle that has formed around us. Attention from so many people causes a tingle of nerves to skate up my spine but also warms my blood. As much as I hated the constant criticism and feelings of failure, a part of me misses performing.

Spurred on by the wild cheering and clapping, I allow Pepe to pick me up and spin me around. His breath is warm on my cheek, his kiss tender against my temple. The crowd grows louder, their applause intensifying as Pepe sets me down, twirling me several times, and dipping me low.

Momentarily hanging upside down, I lock onto the deep blue gaze of Lorenzo.

My breath catches in my throat, my eyes widening as he steps forward.

His eyes glint with an edge I've never detected, his mouth pulled into a firm line. His jawline hardens and his shoulders tense as he glares at me.

Pepe pulls me back up, the smile dying on his lips as he notes Lorenzo's presence over my shoulder. "Can I help you?" he asks Lorenzo in clipped Italian.

The air around us crackles.

"Mia, I need a minute." Lorenzo's fingers encircle my wrist as he jostles me away from Pepe and over to the bar.

Turning over my shoulder, I indicate that I'll only be a moment.

"You won't be going back to him."

"Excuse me?" I try to yank my wrist from Lorenzo's grasp, but he tightens his hold, ignoring me.

Stepping up to the bar, he orders a bottle of water and a shot of vodka. Uncapping the water, he thrusts it into my hands. "Drink."

Tossing back his shot, he hisses, his Adam's apple bobbing, his eyes screwed closed.

I sip the water tentatively. The heat rolling off of Lorenzo's frame is heady, drawing me closer while warning me away.

When he opens his eyes, the anger in them has darkened into a hunger I'm unprepared for and I stumble back a step.

"This club, it's not for you." He growls, his eyes sweeping over me. "What the hell are you doing here?"

## LORENZO

Fucking Mia.

At *this* club. Guys come here to get laid and pry on the innocence and naivety of foreign girls, the study abroad and exchange types. This isn't a place for her. She's too damn good to dance in the center of the club with some douchebag. For God's sake, she recites Petrarca's sonnets and cries when she reads Dante.

Anger rolls down my spine, my fingers clenching into fists, as I think about what could have happened if I wasn't here. Would she have kissed that stronzo? Or worse, gone home with him?

Turning my gaze to her, my breath catches in my throat. She's intoxicatingly gorgeous, even as her eyes shoot daggers at me, her shoulders tensing. "What are you doing here?" I repeat.

"Having a night out with Lexi. Why?"

"I'm just surprised to see you here."

She snorts, rolling her eyes. "Didn't think I ever go out or have a life outside of studying?"

Exasperation rolls through me as I shake my head.

*Yes, that's partly what I thought.*

But the other part of me, the larger part, is furious that she's here in the arms of another man.

*You're mine.*

The words sit on the tip of my tongue, but I swallow them back, knowing how insane they are. Insane and unfair, considering I had Francesca's mouth wrapped around my dick hours ago.

Pinching the bridge of my nose, I spit out. "Most of the guys who here are just looking for a … you know, a one-night thing."

"Is that why you're here?"

I hesitate too long before answering and her neck snaps up. "No."

"Right." She nods, chewing the corner of her mouth. "Well, it was nice seeing you, but I need to find Lexi. Enjoy your night." Her voice is too sharp, her eyes are too unfocused.

Reaching out, I wrap my hand around her wrist. "Have a drink with me." The desperation in my tone is evident, hanging between us like a boundary I'm ready to cross.

Mia turns, her eyes widening, bleeding with a suscepti-bility that soothes my ego and causes my skin to tingle with awareness.

"Please, Mia. Just, stay with me."

"Lexi will —"

"Come find you. I won't let anything happen to you."

"That's not what I'm afraid of." She whispers, a delicious pink blooming in her cheeks.

Furrowing my eyebrows, I step closer, my fingertips pressing into the warmth of her side. "What are you afraid of, bellezza?"

"You." She whispers, her eyes lingering on my lips before latching onto mine.

"I'd never hurt you." I grip her closer, my hand splayed across her hip.

She shakes her head, one side of her mouth lifting and falling.

"You don't trust me?"

"I don't know you."

"Do you want to know me?"

Her eyes glitter, vulnerable and deep and so fucking beautiful. Slowly, she nods. "That's the part that scares me."

*She knows. She already knows I'll ruin her.*

*She knows she's too damn good for the bullshit games I play.*

Tucking a piece of hair behind her ear, she shivers. Closing her eyes, she leans into my palm as I cup her cheek, my thumb brushing a line down the center of her chin.

*Let her go.*

Staring at her, tracing the curves of her cheekbones, counting her long eyelashes, I know it's a lost cause.

I'm already in too deeply.

Want her too badly.

Need her too desperately.

Dipping my head, my lips feather over hers. "Come with me, bellezza."

Her eyes dart up to mine, uncertainty flickering in their depths as she draws in a breath.

"Okay."

# 8

# MIA

"Where are we going?" I ask, stumbling over the rough cobblestones lining the street for the second time.

I'm drunk.

Drunky.

Drunken.

Damn it.

And Lexi encouraged me to leave with Lorenzo. Where is her adherence to the buddy system?

"I got you, Mia." He tightens his hold on my waist, tugging me closer into his side.

Other than that, he doesn't call me out for straight up sucking at holding my alcohol. *Lightweight*, the girls call me. If only it was true.

Arriving at Angelina's, Lorenzo peers down at me, a smile tugging at his lips. "Have a seat anywhere you'd like."

"What?" I ask, blinking as he flips on the lights and neat rows of tables with red-and-white checkered tablecloths appear.

"You need to eat. Something substantial." He quirks an eyebrow at me.

"What are you talking about?" I sit on the nearest chair.

"I mean, not a salad. You need to eat real food." He disappears into the kitchen, returning moments later with a pitcher of water. "Water, Mia."

While Lorenzo is busy in the kitchen, I pour myself a glass of water and study the inside of the restaurant. The place has a rustic charm: old, weather-beaten hardwood floors, black-and-white photographs lining the walls. It looks just like a family-owned Italian restaurant is supposed to and it feels like an extension of someone's kitchen, filled with warmth.

"I hope you like spicy." Lorenzo reemerges from the kitchen with two heaping plates of penne all'arrabiata. Setting the dishes down on one of the tables, he pulls my chair out for me. "Mia."

Charmed by his antics, I grin, sliding into the seat. "Grazie."

If only the girls could see me now, they would be jumping up and down, clapping, dancing, popping bottles. Like an awkward GIF.

"Buon appetito." His eyes drop to my plate and I pick up my fork.

"Buon appetito," I spear a penne onto a tine, my fork hovering in the air.

*How many grams of carbs is one penne?*

*Is this whole wheat?*

*How many hours of ballet combinations would it take to burn off this plate of pasta?*

Lorenzo clears his throat, watching me expectantly.

I flush, bringing the penne to my mouth. "Mmm. This is delicious," And, damn it to hell, it is. The sauce is perfect—just spicy enough to have a kick but not enough to induce coughing. "Thank you."

"You're welcome." He takes a huge bite. "Do you like to cook?"

Pushing the pasta around my plate, hiding penne underneath heaps of sauce, anxiety swells in my chest. *How am I supposed to eat all of this? Oh God, does he expect me to finish it all?* "A bit. I'm not good at it or anything, but I find it relaxing. Do you?" *This is easily more than three servings.*

"I've never really tried it. I know a few of the staples we serve in case I have to jump in and help but Mama always cooked growing up."

I chew another penne. *Slow down, Mia.*

"So, what are you majoring in?" he asks.

"Is this a date?" I blurt out, mentally slapping myself. Twice.

"No." Lorenzo chuckles, chewing another bite.

*Why do I suck at this? Why did I ask him that?* My face must be as red as Mars in this moment and —

"I don't, I don't really do dates. But I'd like to know you better."

"Why?"

Lorenzo smirks. "You never say what I think you're going to."

"Neither do you."

"Why do I want to know you?"

I nod, biting my tongue. Sometimes, it's best for me to stay silent.

"Because you're —"

"Unexpected?" Gah! Stop talking!

"Special."

I roll my eyes even though his words warm up the hollow places in my chest. *Does he really believe that?* Or — "I expected more of an original line from you."

Lorenzo laughs, swiping a hand along his jaw. Nodding,

he admits, "You're right. But that wasn't a line; I do think you're special."

I stuff a penne in my mouth.

"I like you. You're different, captivating, confusing as hell."

I snort, some of my embarrassment easing. *Does he really like me? Or does he just like flirting?*

"I like the way you murmur to yourself when you read in Italian. I like how Petrarca's sonnets cause tears to stick to your eyelashes. You chew the corner of your mouth when something affects you and your eyes blaze with fire when I piss you off. I like how you still haven't messaged me even though I beg you to nearly every day."

"I still don't need help." I laugh.

"You're unlike every woman I know. You're refreshing and challenging and so goddamn sweet you scare the hell out of me."

*Wait, what?*

My heart stops.

I'm dead.

Lorenzo Barca, frowning, glaring, charming Enzo, former professional race car driver, Italian heartthrob, and pusher of carbohydrates, likes me.

Really *likes* me.

The virgin from New York who doesn't know how to flirt.

And he doesn't know what to do about it.

Hell, I don't know what to do about it.

"I don't say things like this, Mia. To anyone."

I narrow my eyes.

"You don't believe me?"

Shrugging, I admit, "I remember the way you flirted with that woman the first day I met you. And then, tonight at the club, the girl with the green eyes who was all over you."

Lorenzo frowns. "Caterina? She means nothing."

"Really?"

Sighing, he pinches the bridge of his nose. "My social circle is convoluted. And not worth knowing. Those women, they're nothing like you."

*Ain't that the truth.*

"Tonight, when I saw you dancing with that guy," Lorenzo looks away, his jaw straining, "Jesu, it pissed me off."

*Say what? Repeat, repeat!*

"I don't date for real or do relationships, Mia."

*What God giveth, God taketh away.*

And now I'm quoting the Bible.

"But with you, I want to." Lorenzo's fingers curl around mine, holding my hand. "Give me a shot, bellezza. Go out with me."

"Okay." I say slowly.

"Good. Now finish eating so I can take you home."

Huh? Confusion rocks through me. "To your house?"

He shakes his head, brushing a piece of hair off of my face. "Trust me, bellezza, I'm desperate to take you to my house, peel off your clothes, and keep you pinned to my bed until morning."

I'm dying again. A slow and torturous death. Because Lorenzo's *words* make me feel things, sensations I'm not sure what to do with. Pressing my thighs together under the table, I shift. Pulling my hair over my left shoulder, the cool air that hits my neck is a relief.

"But you've been drinking. Heavily. And when I take you, Mia, you're going to remember every single second of it."

Inhaling sharply, my fingers clench the tablecloth.

Lorenzo's eyes darken to midnight, an insatiable hunger

glinting.

"I think I should go now." I whisper.

Lorenzo holds my gaze for a beat before nodding. "I'll walk you home."

---

"AND HE DIDN'T KISS you? What the hell!" Emma's face flashes across my computer screen.

"Are you speechless? Did I render chatterbox Emma Stanton speechless? I'm awesome!"

"I'm surprised is all."

"That I was asked on a date? Um, thanks."

"No! That you called me before Maura."

"Ah, to be honest, I feel guilty about it."

"Don't. Everyone knows I give the best reactions."

"Hence, my call. Now, tell me what you think."

"About your date? Or the non-kiss?"

"Both."

"Babe, the date's going to be awesome. Wear something sexy, have a glass of wine before you go, and enjoy yourself."

I roll my eyes. This is why no one calls Emma for advice. She sucks at it.

"And, for the non-kiss, it's because he likes you. Like, for real."

"Right?" I ask, too excited that she's confirming my suspicions. "I take back everything I just thought about you."

Emma laughs. "Rome is good for you Mia. Or maybe it's just getting out from under the rigor of ballet. But you look incredible, all happy and shiny. And you seem…different."

*What does that mean and why does everyone keep using it as my number one descriptor?*

"Different how?"

"More confident, less insecure. Badass."

"I'll take it."

"So, tell me about this Italiano."

"He's," I sigh, pursing my lips as I try to describe Lorenzo, "all the things. Sexy and arrogant. Smart and witty. All-consuming, all-knowing, I can't even think when I'm with him." I cover my eyes with one hand as I blush.

"Oh my God! He's God!"

"What?"

"Omniscient, omnipotent, and omnipresent."

"Stop. Please, just stop." I shake my head but I'm laughing. In the small box where I can see my face on the screen, I'm glowing. Emma's right; I am happy.

"I'm freaking proud of you, Mia. You have to tell Lila; she's going to die."

"No, wait. Don't tell anyone yet. I'm not even sure what's actually happening here. I need to go on the date first. And see if he kisses me. Oh my God. What if things don't work out? Do you think I ruined my study spot and I need to start scouting options to read Dante and drink caffè lattes?"

Emma snorts. "Relax. You're fine. You definitely don't have to find a new study spot. Just see what happens. Go on the date, be your normal self, don't act weird, and just see where everything between the two of you leads."

"Me, normal? I'm freaking out here."

"I know, but this is a good thing, Mia. You accepted a date with a hot Italiano after dancing the night away with a different hot Italiano. Just have fun. You said you wanted to do this study abroad because of how much your mom wanted you to travel, enjoy life, have experiences. So go, enjoy, make out, live! Don't complicate it overanalyzing. You had an awesome Saturday night. Done."

"You're right."

"I know."

"What's new by you?"

"Nothing really. Going to brunch with my new roomies tomorrow."

"What? You're cheating on us!"

She chuckles. "Shh, don't tell the other girls. It will be fun though. A nice chance for all of us to catch up on our week. I barely see my roommates with how busy I am here."

"Knowing you, that sounds about right." Emma is always super involved. In everything.

"Anyway, love, I've got to go. I'm so glad to see your sunny face and hear about how you're killing it in Roma. Keep me posted on Lorenzo deets. And make sure you call Lila soon. She's a smitten kitten about Cade and wants to gush about him all the time."

"I know, but I'm happy she's with him. I'll catch up with her soon. Thanks for listening. Enjoy brunch tomorrow."

"Thanks. Love you."

"Love you too. Ciao."

"See ya." Emma clicks off, her face momentarily frozen on screen before disappearing.

Falling back onto my bed, I check the time. 3:40AM.

Staring at my ceiling, the sticky heat of the night coating my skin, my stomach grumbles. Ugh. I feel ill from how much alcohol I consumed tonight. Followed by pasta. Looking down at the swollen bulge of my stomach, I screw my eyes closed.

*Don't think about it.*

I can't help it. After tossing and turning for fifteen minutes, I make my way down the hall and into the bathroom. Once my system is purged, I feel better. Lighter.

*Lorenzo: Buona notte, bellezza.*

Re-reading Lorenzo's message, I fall asleep smiling.

# 9

# MIA

L orenzo: You never told me, what are you majoring in?
    Me: Dance.

Lorenzo: Seriously?

Me: Surprised?

Lorenzo: Impressed. I saw the way you moved at the club.

Me: (Dancing woman in the red dress emoji x 5)

Lorenzo: You're sexier.

Me: (Laughing emoji x 5)

Lorenzo: If you didn't major in dance, what would you have chosen?

Me: Astronomy.

Lorenzo: For real?

Me: Totally. What about you?

Lorenzo: Majored in business.

Me: That worked out well.

Lorenzo: Depends on how you look at it.

Me: ???

Lorenzo: Visit me at Angelina's on Monday?

Me: Duh.

Lorenzo: ???

*Me: I'll be there.*

---

"HOW ARE YOU FEELING TODAY?" Lorenzo grins at me as I slide into my usual seat on the patio of Angelina's.

"Still hungover." I hold my thumb and pointer finger an inch apart. "A little bit."

"You mixed too many different kinds of alcohol."

"Tell me about it."

"Do you remember our conversation?"

Flipping my sunglasses on top of my head, I wince as the sunlight assaults me; I'm not cut out for heavy drinking. "The part where you asked me out on a proper date?"

Lorenzo smirks, a flash of color rippling across his face.

"Oh my God. Are you embarrassed?" I reach out and squeeze his wrist.

He slips into the chair beside mine, leaning back. "I don't really do dates."

"So you've said."

Nodding, he bites his lower lip, looking at me through narrowed eyes. "Wine or history?"

"What?" I snort. "That's like comparing apples to oranges."

"It's not a direct comparison. I'm asking which you like better. Don't think, just answer."

"Both."

Lorenzo looks toward the sky, chuckling. "I don't know why I thought a simple question would be easy with you. Okay, wine or cheese?"

"Wine."

"City or country?"

"City."

"Vintage or new?"

"Vintage."

Lorenzo leans closer, his hand cupping the side of my cheek. "You don't have classes on Friday, right?"

I shake my head, turning my face to press a kiss in the palm of his hand.

Lorenzo shifts closer, dropping his voice. "I'll pick you up for our date at ten."

"In the morning?" My eyes snap up to his. "Where are we going?"

"It's a surprise."

"How come that wasn't one of your questions? I don't like surprises."

Lorenzo stands from his chair. Bending down, he kisses both of my cheeks, lingering a beat too long.

The energy between us shifts, the sounds of the street fading into background noise. Hooking a finger underneath my chin, he lifts my face to his, his eyes dark, swirling with an intensity I don't understand but latch onto. "Friday." He whispers and I'm not sure if he's speaking to me or himself.

"Friday."

---

"Wow! I'm dying to know where he is taking you on your date." Lila's cornflower blue eyes and bright blond hair light up my screen.

"You're literally glowing." I tell her.

"I think I'm in love."

"I think you are too. Tell me about Cade."

"No way; I've been telling everyone about Cade every time we talk. Tell me about the Italiano."

"There's not much to tell. We're going on a date Friday. But he hasn't even kissed me yet."

"He will. And then, he's going to try and lock you down."

"No, he's not. I think I'm the first girl he's ever asked on a real date."

"That means he really likes you. Think about it, he could probably have any woman he wants and —"

"He wants the socially awkward virgin?"

"Uh-uh. Don't do that."

I raise my eyebrows as Lila's face grows stern.

"Don't slam yourself. You're not nearly as socially awkward as you once were. And I credit myself for that."

I laugh, nodding because she's right. When I first started at McShain, my entire world was ballet. I barely knew how to interact with people outside of my dance studio. Little by little, Lila, Emma, and Maura drew me out, introduced me to parties and socializing, bolstered my confidence, supported my fumbling steps into adulthood.

"Does he know you're a virgin?"

I shake my head. "How do you even tell a guy that? I mean, it would be different if we were in some serious relationship or I knew he had only been with a few women but this guy," I shake my head, "he's the total opposite of any guy I've ever gone out with or kissed."

"Good. You need someone who's going to take control, focus on you, light you up like —"

"Okay." I raise my hand. "I get your point. But, do I tell him?"

Lila wrinkles her nose. "You kind of have to. That's a messed-up thing to not tell a guy before you do it. Do you want to have sex with him?"

Blushing, I lift my hand to my cheek as Lila laughs.

"That's a hell yeah, isn't it?"

I nod.

"Good for you, Mia. I'm meeting Kristen and Sam for drinks now but please, please message me all about your date. And have so much fun."

"Thanks Li. You too."

"Talk soon."

"Ciao bella."

---

THE REMAINDER of the week passes quickly as I throw myself into schoolwork, hanging out with Lexi, and family dinners with Paola and Gianluca.

On Thursday evening, Gianluca teaches Lexi and me how to make gnocchi.

"Don't tell my mom you taught me this, Gianluca. She'll start forcing me to cook for all her dinner parties." Lexi takes a sip of her wine, gesturing toward the three balls of dough on top of the table.

"Cara, I feel like you are drinking more than you are working." Gianluca says.

"Fair point. I am my mother's daughter after all." Lexi smirks, refilling our wine glasses.

"Okay, Mia, for this part, we need to roll the dough out into a long rope." Gianluca explains, showing me how to roll out the dough.

Getting to work, I follow his lead while Lexi continues to sip her wine and oversee our progress.

"I really want to know where he's taking you tomorrow." Lexi comments off-handedly.

Gianluca smirks. "A hot date?"

"Lorenzo finally asked her out."

"Lorenzo Barca?" Gianluca asks, an undercurrent in his

tone.

"Yes. See, I told you I would hook her up with him."

I roll my eyes.

"Where are you guys going, cara?" Gianluca directs his question to me.

"I'm not sure, it's a surprise."

"Hm."

"What?" I ask, using the back of my hand to scratch my nose since my fingers are covered in flour and bits of dough.

"Just be careful, Mia."

I nod but of course, Lexi is curious. "Why? You think he's playing her?"

"Thanks Lexi." I toss some flour at her.

Gianluca shakes his head, "I don't know. It's unfair to judge someone by their reputation alone but Enzo, he has one. I just don't want to see you get hurt, Mia."

"What happened to falling in lust and embracing Roma?" Lexi boosts herself to sit on the countertop, her legs swinging.

"That was before I knew Mia was dating Enzo Barca."

---

GIANLUCA'S WARNING echoes in my mind the next morning as I dress for my date with Lorenzo. Taking time to curl the ends of my hair and apply makeup, I slip into a simple light blue dress that flares at my waist. With buttons from the neckline to the hem, the dress reminds me of classic 1950's Italian fashion. Twirling in front of my mirror, I giggle.

I've never been so excited for a date before.

Donning silver sandals, I grab my purse and sunglasses and leave my bedroom.

"Cara, wait." Gianluca's voice rings out as I make my way to the front door.

Turning, he offers me a grin. "You look beautiful."

"Thank you."

"I'm sorry if I seemed harsh yesterday; it was unfair of me to make any assumptions about your relationship with Enzo."

"Gianluca, it's okay. It's a first date." I slide my purse onto my shoulder.

He stuffs his hands into his pockets, rocking from his heels to his toes and back again. "Still. Have fun. Just remember that you deserve the world, and any guy that isn't willing to give that to you isn't worth your time. Va bene?"

"Va bene. And thank you, for looking out for me."

"You're like my daughter, cara." He jokes but then his eyes turn serious. "You're the sensible one while she," he thumbs toward Lexi's bedroom door, "is the wild child. When the sensible, sweet girl has her heart broken for the first time, it never heals right again." He nods once. "Now go, he's waiting."

# 10

# LORENZO

W atching Mia step out from behind the big green door, my breath lodges in my throat.

She's breathtaking.

When she looks up and sees me leaning against the 1967 Alfa Romeo 33 Stradale, her face transforms. Brown eyes widening, full lips parting, a wave of awe washing over her features.

"No way." She grins. "Where did you get this car?"

"It's my Papa's. You said vintage." I remind her, holding open the passenger door so she can slip inside.

Sliding behind the steering wheel, I flip the ignition and guide the car out of the city limits. "You ready for this?"

"Where are we going?"

"You really dislike surprises."

Mia shrugs, but her eyes glitter; she's enjoying the surprise more than she wants to admit.

"We have about two-and-a-half hours of driving." I reach over and place a hand on her thigh.

"Is that my first clue? Or are you telling me to get comfortable?"

"Both."

She smirks, settling back into her seat.

"You look beautiful, Mia."

"You clean up pretty well yourself."

Chuckling, I brush my fingers over the soft material of her dress, wondering how her bare skin would feel. Feminine, dainty, sweet, Mia reminds me of a porcelain doll. But then she turns her wickedly dark eyes in my direction and my doll transforms into a seductress.

At least where I'm concerned.

Wanting her the way I do is a slow, sweet torture.

Because I'm desperate for her to let me in, to pull me close, but at the same time, I know that men like me only ruin good girls like her.

And I don't want to ruin Mia.

I want to answer the riddles of her mind, understand the complexities of her heart, and watch her body light up and explode like a firecracker.

"You okay?" Mia's voice pulls me from my thoughts.

"Yeah, sorry, just thinking. How are you enjoying Roma?"

"It's everything."

I snicker. "What's the even mean?"

Mia grins, her teeth sinking into her bottom lip. "I don't know if I'll explain it well but it's just, life. Bright colors and sharp sounds, a history I want to lose myself in and a future I want to belong to. I adore the people I've met here, the warmth of the culture, the beauty of the language. It's almost like it's not real; like I could never keep it forever. Does that make sense?"

I nod, understanding the depth of her feelings for the city I call home. "It's a special place."

"It's more than that. Or maybe, it's just me when I'm here."

"What do you mean?"

"I'm a dancer. *Was* a dancer. Ballerina Mia."

Catching her fingers in mine, I lace our hands together. "Tutus and tight hair buns?"

"All of it."

"Were you any good?"

She scoffs and I chuckle. "Kidding bellezza, I'm sure you are good at everything you do."

"Hardly." She shakes her head. "But yes, I excelled at ballet. It was my whole world." Her voice dips, an edge of bitterness hugging her words.

"What do you mean?"

"It's competitive. There are so few spots available in ballet companies, and then the hierarchy within them is nearly impossible. You must be perfect all of the time. Every combination, flawless, the column of your neck, graceful, the extension of your arms, correct. There is no room for error. No room to have a bad day or feel unwell or gain a pound. It's classes and honing technique and staying one step ahead of everyone else."

Turning to her, I'm surprised she's facing the window, her voice low as if she's recounting a memory.

"I was the best in my year. A shining star. And I breathed ballet. Every decision, how I dressed, what I ate, how I walked all contributed to my passion. I wanted to dance for the American Ballet Theater; it was my dream."

"What happened?" I interject, my fingers squeezing hers as her hand grows cold in mine.

"Six months ago, I was injured. I landed wrong from a grand jeté. The moment before, I was perfect, suspended in air like a marvel. Like magic. My posture was spot on, no tension in my neck, my arms graceful, toes pointed." She trails off, shaking her head. "Anyway, I tore my ACL and that was the end of it."

My chest tightens at her words, my heart sinking at her tone. Distant, like she doesn't care, which is a lie. I glimpsed the emotions that crossed her face when she spoke about her dream, her passion, and they were real. Raw. "Have you thought about rehabilitation and physical —"

She unlinks our fingers, holding up her hand. "Trust me, it's over. And maybe it's better this way."

"Why would you say that? You clearly loved ballet, yearned to be a part of this theater."

She nods, "I did. For so long, I did. But I never got to do things like this." She gestures between us.

"Date?"

"Just, be. Take a road trip on a Friday morning to explore, stay up late with my friends watching a movie, drink wine in the middle of the week because I feel like it. I loved dancing so much I didn't realize I gave up my freedom."

"Okay, but couldn't you have both?"

The corner of her mouth ticks up and she nods. "Sure, you can definitely have both. But not if you want to be the best, number one. And I couldn't settle for less than that."

"Ah, you're competitive."

"With myself."

"I understand."

"Do you?" she raises a skeptical eyebrow.

"Yes. After Papa died, I went on a bender of sorts. Drinking, drugs, hard partying all night, every night. I screwed up all of my qualifying races, lost out on the F1 Circuit." I tap the heel of my palm against the steering wheel, agitated by my own short-sightedness, my own stupidity. "And since then, I've been trying to prove to myself that I still have it, can still beat out all competition. I've been reckless: street racing, racing for pink slips, totaling my last Maserati. But I miss the adrenaline, the hype, the … freedom. In a different sense than you mean. The way I feel when I'm racing is unlike anything else; now that I don't have racing, it's like I'm constantly chasing a high but always falling short. I need to know I can get it back."

"Damn." Mia whispers. "I'm sorry, Lorenzo. That sucks. Are you going to work toward it again?"

"Absolutely." I grip the steering wheel, feeling a renewed connection to my old life, a spark that I've been missing these past few months. "Are you?"

Mia tilts her head before shaking it slowly. "No. I've gained more since ballet ended. It's been a really hard transition, most days I feel like I'm failing, but I think I'm going to be okay."

"You're always going to be okay, Mia."

She shakes her head, her eyes flickering with vulnerability. "How can you be so sure?"

"Control freaks like you are always okay."

She snorts, swatting my arm.

"No, seriously, you'll be okay because the worst has already happened. You've lost your dream but you're here, creating a new one. Because you want to, because you choose to. That means you're already okay."

"I guess so."

"Hey," I palm her thigh. "You're more than okay, Mia Petrella. You're smart and thoughtful, passionate and inquisitive. You're so bright and beautiful, you block out everything around you; you're like looking at the sun."

She rolls her eyes but her mouth splits into a smile. "I

think without ballet, it's like I finally have room, space, to become myself."

"Then keep doing you, Mia. The rest will sort itself out."

"Hope so."

"Know so."

# 11

# MIA

"Oh my God. Is this Siena? Are we going to Siena?" I ask, leaning forward in my seat until my nose practically touches the windshield.

Rolling hills and cypress trees surround us as we pass a sign indicating the city is twelve kilometers away.

A grin flickers across Lorenzo's mouth as he nods.

"Oh my God!" I exclaim, clasping my hands together and dropping back in my seat. "I can't believe it!"

"You said city."

"I wasn't expecting Siena. I wasn't expecting any of this." I slide my hand over the soft leather of the car's interior.

"I'm glad I'm delivering on the surprise portion."

"Lorenzo, you're delivering on everything."

He winks devilishly, his eyes assessing me with a flicker of heat. "You haven't seen anything yet, bellezza."

———

SIENA OPENS before us like a fan. A medieval city comprised

of beautiful architecture, exquisite art spanning centuries, and of course, mouth-watering cuisine.

Twirling in the Piazza del Campo, the sun heats my face as my eyes jump from one architectural marvel to another. "There is where they hold the Palio, isn't it?"

"Si. The Palio di Siena is held twice a year, in July and August. Ten riders from different parts of the city race and wear the colors to represent their contrade, or ward. It is incredible. You will have to return here." Lorenzo laces his fingers with mine, tugging me down a side street. "Siena reveres Madonna, Jesus's mother Mary. Here," he points to the top of a building on the corner of a street, "you will see her painted throughout the city to guard travelers on their journey."

"Like little street shrines."

"Exactly."

Walking hand in hand down the tiny medieval streets, Lorenzo pauses to point out interesting historical or artistic facts. Hanging onto his every word, he's like my own private guide of the city.

Once we re-enter the Piazza del Campo, he pulls me toward a high tower. "Come on, you have to see the Cappella di Piazza, it's a small chapel but dedicated to La Madonna and then, we will climb the Torre del Mangia. From the top, we will have the most beautiful views of the city."

Falling into step with Lorenzo, I soak up the information he shares, breathe in the energy he exudes, and fall just a little bit in love with this surprise lover of the arts. Glancing up at him, with streams of sunlight radiating around him, his strong jawline and brilliant eyes on display, it's hard to believe that he is here with me.

That he planned the most perfect first date for me.

His swagger, the confidence he exudes, rendered me speechless the first time we met.

But now, I'm in awe of *him*. Sophisticated and intelligent, passionate and bold, witty and entertaining, Lorenzo is all the things. And he's so sexy, so unbelievably sensual, that just looking at him causes my mouth to grow dry, my skin to tingle with awareness.

I've never craved a man's touch the way I crave his. I never dreamt to be kissed the way I yearn for his lips to cover mine. I never cared one way or the other that I am the oldest living virgin I know. But damn, do I want to give my virginity to Lorenzo.

"You okay, bellezza?" he squeezes my hand.

His blue eyes gleam, amusement tugging on the corners of his mouth.

Nodding, I reach up and slowly wrap my fingers around the back of his neck. Rolling onto my toes, I press my lips against his.

If Lorenzo is surprised, he doesn't let on. In fact, after the initial pressure of my mouth against his, he tugs me flush against his frame and palms the center of my back.

He kisses me softly, once, twice, before taking control of the exchange. Lacing his fingers through my hair, his fingertips clutch the back of my head. Moaning, my lips part and Lorenzo's tongue slips inside, meeting mine.

The stubble from his chin scrapes against mine, rooting me to the moment as his scent, spicy cologne and fresh basil and something uniquely Lorenzo, pulls me under.

My hands grip his biceps, traveling upward to his shoulders. Rocking into him, he picks me up and walks us into a tiny alcove, tucked between the business of the Campo and the quietness of surrounding neighborhoods.

"Mia," he whispers against my mouth. My name is like a prayer on his lips.

My head drops back against the brick building he holds me against as his mouth moves to my neck, suckling and nipping and working me over.

"Jesu, I want you more than I want my next breath."

My eyes fall closed as the sound of our mingled panting fills my ears.

Lorenzo's hands are roving, one gripping my hip, the other traveling underneath my dress, sliding up my leg until

—

"Fuck, bellezza. We can't do this here. Not like this. I want to savor you, take my time. Please, God, give me patience." He mutters to himself, dropping his forehead to my shoulder.

My eyes pop open as I stare up at the bright blue sky, half-delirious with want for this man. Steadying my breathing, I nod. He's right. I know he is. My first time should not be outside, up against a medieval structure, in broad daylight.

Sliding down his frame, my body shivers from the friction.

*Oh God. Now what do I do? Say? How do I act?*

"Come." Lorenzo's voice is huskier than usual, demanding. "You said wine."

---

I'M quiet on the drive to wherever we're going next.

How could I not be? I am so out of my comfort zone here.

My body is desperate for Lorenzo to touch and explore and kiss. My mind is a whirlwind of contradicting thoughts and overflowing insecurities.

*If he didn't stop, would I have had sex with him? Outside? In public?*

*Do I want to have sex with him?*

*Should I have sex with him?*

*Today? Or later, like after our first date?*

*Are we going to go on another date?*

*Does this mean more to me than it does to him?*

*Probably. It has to.*

*I mean, I'm the virgin.*

*Gah! I wish I could use a lifeline and call a friend.*

*Who would I call?*

*Probably Maura.*

*Although Emma would have the most priceless reaction.*

*But this is so much more of Lila's expertise. She'd give the best advice.*

*Oh my God, who cares? I can't call anyone!*

*Should I have sex with Lorenzo?*

"Bellezza." His voice carries a hint of amusement as his palm grazes my thigh. "What are you thinking about?"

Gah! *What do I say? I think I want you to take my virginity, but I don't want to end up overly attached to some free-loving former F1 driver?*

"Mia, you can tell me anything. Was that, too much, back there?" His eyebrows draw together, the palm on my thigh stilling.

I clear my throat. *Just tell him, Mia!*

Looking over at him, concern shades his eyes.

Shaking my head, I smile. "No, I'm fine."

# 12

# LORENZO

I don't push Mia when she tells me she's fine.

Even though I'm not sure if she's being honest.

Hell yeah, I've hooked up with countless women against countless city streets. But I'd never do something like that with Mia. At least, not the first time we get together.

Jesu, the first time I kiss the girl and I've got her pinned up against a chapel. But her sweetness is intoxicating; it riles me up more than if she did a goddamn striptease. When I'm with her, I lose my head, forget how I'm supposed to act, and just *feel*. The realization scares the hell out of me. Because it's a different type of reckless than the drinking and partying. This type of reckless could ruin me. Not my career or my reputation but *me*.

Mia Petrella could own my heart and claim my soul and I'd give it freely. Without thinking twice.

Which are feelings I've never experienced before and they are heady in their magnitude, sharp in their intensity.

Turning down the long road that leads to my family's vineyard, I glance at Mia.

I watch her expression as the road curves and the long row of cypress trees greet us.

A gasp falls from her lips as a sign bearing my family name comes into view. She turns to me, her eyes wide, her mouth gaping.

"You said wine."

---

"CIAO, ENZO. HOW ARE YOU?" Matteo, our head vintner, shakes my hand. "I'm happy you called; there's a lot we need to discuss."

Nodding, I glance at Mia. "Today, I'm here in a more personal capacity."

"Ah." Matteo nods, smiling at Mia. "Pleasure to meet you. I'm Matteo."

"Mia." Mia shakes his hand. "I've never been to a vineyard before."

"Oh, well then you're in for a great afternoon. Let me give you a tour." Matteo's eyes cut to me. "Next week, please, we need to talk."

"Of course."

"Come Mia. Let me show you around. Here, we make Nobile di Montepulciano, created mostly from the Sangiovese grape. Don't confuse our wine with the Montepulciano variety from Abruzzo…" The next hour consists of a tour around the vineyard with detailed explanations from Matteo.

Following Matteo and Mia around, I smile at the emotions flitting over Mia's face. Curiosity, wonder, excitement, confusion, understanding. She asks specific questions, which delights Matteo, makes small talk with various staff, and after sixty-minutes, has a legion of fans.

Drawing her away from her admirers, I promise to call Matteo next week. Leading Mia down into the cellar, a table with several glasses and bottles of wine for tasting is already set up.

"Wow, Lorenzo, this is beautiful."

"I know."

"Oh my God. Quit staring at me." She laughs, pushing my shoulder.

Tilting my head toward the table, Mia and I sit, tasting wine and nibbling on cheese, chocolates, and an assortment of snacks.

"This one is bolder." She smirks, placing down her glass.

"Becoming a wine connoisseur?"

"Hardly. I just know what I like."

"So do I."

She snorts, blushing.

Leaning over, I move her wine glass out of the way and shift closer to Mia.

Her eyes widen, dark as midnight, dropping to my lips.

"I'm going to kiss you now and this time, I'm not going to stop unless you tell me to." My words are rough, rounded out with emotion.

For the past hour, I suffered. Watching her laugh and joke with Matteo and other staff, noting her easygoing smile, the sincerity in her eyes, and not being able to touch her the way I wanted to was torture. With each passing step, every question she asked, I wanted to cover her mouth with mine, hear her sweet moan again.

And now, now it is finally time.

We are alone in the cellar. A rustic atmosphere with old wood and red brick, the lights are dimmed, the mood is ripe. No one will interrupt us. And I don't want to let this moment slip away.

"Okay." Her voice is soft, hesitant.

Frowning, I tuck a strand of hair behind her ear. "Mia, I —"

But she surprises me again.

Leaning over the armrest of her chair, she arches her neck and brushes her lips against mine.

And all thoughts evaporate.

She tastes like heaven and hell, my salvation and damnation.

Her mouth is sweet with bursts of cherry and blackberry from the wine, her lips soft, her skin smooth. She gasps, that tiny groan dropping from her lips and I'm lost to this moment. To her.

Tugging her forward, she shifts to my chair, kneeling on either side of my hips, her thighs gripping mine. I shift back in my seat, pulling her forward, until her tiny frame melts into me.

Her hands clamp down on my shoulders, her hair falling around us like a curtain, blocking out the dim light until we're wrapped in our own bubble.

Kissing her with abandon, I grip her waist, sliding one palm upward, along her tiny frame, my fingers traveling over her ribcage, over the swell of her breast, around to the neckline of her dress.

A trail of buttons has never seemed so challenging before, but I manage to pop open enough for her breasts to spill out. Moaning, I break our kiss to draw one of her perfect breasts into my mouth, my tongue lapping at her nipple.

She freezes under my touch, her fingers digging into the skin of my shoulder blades.

"Lorenzo." Her voice is raspy, an edge of panic flaring around my name.

I pause, dragging my eyes up to hers.

"I'm a virgin."

Ice. Water. To. My. Everything.

"What the hell?" I jerk back, pulling her dress over her breasts, my fingers fumbling with the buttons.

"Stop." Her hands swat at mine. Easing off my lap, she turns, walking several paces away.

Her head is bent, her fingers grappling with the buttons, her shoulders trembling.

Shame slams into me; I scared her.

But what the hell?

A virgin?

Standing, I straighten my shirt, run my hand along my jaw. "Mia."

"No, please. Don't say anything." Her voice wavers, tears lacing in her tone.

"Bellezza, please." I close the distance between us, laying a hand on her shoulder.

She freezes, her body locking down.

"I didn't mean to react so harshly."

"Why? You were honest."

"I was surprised."

"See? No one likes surprises."

Smirking, I pull her frame back and wrap my arms around her shoulders. "I do." I whisper into her hair, pressing a kiss to her temple.

Her hands reach up, linking onto my arms folded across the top of her chest. Relieved that she's not pushing me away, I hold her closer. "You caught me off-guard. I knew you were innocent, more so than other girls. But Jesu, Mia, if I'd known you were a virgin, I wouldn't have pressed you up against a church wall, considered laying you down on a table in a wine cellar."

"What if I wanted you to?" Her voice falters, a shiver working down her spine.

"It would have been the moment talking."

"What?"

"You want it in the moment, and I understand that. But as the person with more experience, it's up to me to make sure your first time is special. Significant. And worthy of you."

She spins in my embrace, her soulful eyes latching onto mine. "You want to see me again?"

I chuckle, shaking my head. "Bellezza, do you think I plan days like this, first dates, for any woman? I've never done anything like this in my life. I'm trying to convince you to take a chance on me."

"What? Why? Girls fall at your feet."

"Not the girl I want. Not you."

"So, what? Are we dating?"

"We're doing whatever you want, Mia. From now on, you call the shots. I want you; I want you so badly it aches. But your virginity is a gift and it's up to you to decide if I'm the right man to receive it. Either way, I want to spend time with you, Mia. Know you better."

"Why me?"

Dropping my arms, my hands reach up to frame her face, my thumbs brushing against her cheekbones. "You have no idea, do you? I already told you, bellezza, you're different."

"Different."

"More."

She shakes her head.

I drop my forehead to hers and tell her the truth that fills me with hope and fear. "Mia, you're unraveling my world. Each moment with you shifts the way I see things. I just hope you stick around long enough to spin it into something brighter. Better."

IT'S LATE when I pull in front of the Franchetti's green door. Turning off the ignition, I turn toward Mia and clasp her fingers in mine.

"Mia, today was —"

"Perfect."

I nod. "Thank you for coming with me."

"Thank you for planning the best first date."

"Thank you for being honest with me."

Her cheeks flame red and she covers her face with her hand. "Oh God, let's not talk about that again."

"Don't be embarrassed, bellezza. Please, I'm honored, truly, that you would even consider me."

"Okay, that's enough honesty."

Chuckling, I drop the topic. "See you Monday at Angelina's?"

"Of course. I better go; I feel like Gianluca is peeking out the windows waiting for me."

"Oh, he is. He'll be by Angelina's tomorrow to warn me."

"Warn you?"

"About all the ways he'll hurt me if I break your heart."

"Then don't break it."

"Trust me, bellezza, there's a much greater chance of you breaking mine."

She rolls her eyes, not believing me for a second. But it's the truth. I'm already too far gone, want her too badly, to make it out of this unscathed.

Leaning over, I press a goodnight kiss against her lips.

"Buona notte, bellezza."

"Buona notte, Lorenzo."

OCTOBER

# 13

# MIA

"So, you're like, dating?" Maura asks, her eyes widening over FaceTime.

"Kind of. I mean, Siena was a real date."

"The best first date in the history of life."

"Exactly. But yeah, now we've fallen into this easy rhythm. I stop by Angelina's every afternoon after class. We hang out. And then, when he finishes work, sometimes we meet for a coffee or gelato. We went to a movie last week."

"So, dating."

"Dating." I confirm.

"Wow. He must really like you." Maura whispers.

"God, I hope so. Also, why are you whispering?"

"Because." Her eyes widen as if that explains it.

"Because why?" I widen my eyes back at her.

She giggles and it is the most uncharacteristic sound I've ever heard Maura make that my eyebrows knit together in confusion.

"Because I'm drunk," she hiccups.

"What?" This time my eyes do widen. In surprise, which I hate. And concern.

"Shh. Don't tell anyone. We're technically dry." She waves a hand. Her rowing team is always dry, her coach demanding perfection from his rowers. And alcohol impedes perfection, so Maura rarely drinks. Until now.

"Why are you drinking?" I try to understand her change in behavior. Maura always put rowing before everything else. There is no way she would jeopardize her spot on the team, by getting drunk on a whim.

"Felt like it."

"Okay," I say slowly. "Maura, I—"

"Oh, I have to tell you something important." She cuts me off, her words slurring.

"What's wrong?"

"It's about Lila." She widens her eyes.

"I have no idea what you're trying to tell me with your eyes." I snort. "Is Lila okay?"

Maura shakes her head and fills me in on what's happening with Lila and Cade. I groan, my hand flying up to cover my mouth in shock as memories of my mother's cancer flit through my mind.

Poor Lila. This must be killing her. But really, poor Cade. My heart aches as I think about the challenges he is going to face in the coming weeks. The chemotherapy, the weakening of his body, the loss of his dreams.

When I hang up with Maura, I squeeze my eyes shut and say a prayer for Cade.

Then I FaceTime Lila, hoping to provide her with some support. She looks tired, purple smudges underneath her eyes. Her eyes fill with tears as she tells me about Cade's diagnosis.

After we hang up, a wave of homesickness washes over me.

I miss my friends.

*Me: Hey, what are you up to?*

*Lorenzo: Just locking up at Angelina's. You?*

*Me: Need a distraction.*

*Lorenzo: You okay?*

*Me: I think so.*

*Lorenzo: Did something happen? Is someone bothering you? Are you hurt?*

Rolling my eyes at his overprotectiveness, I tap out a reply.

*Me: No, homesick.*

*Lorenzo: Be there in ten.*

---

"You can't be serious." My heart swells all the way into my throat as I read the seriousness in Lorenzo's eyes.

"You told me about the pact."

"Because we were having a conversation about our friends. And I now wish I didn't."

"You're supposed to be living on the edge."

"Of life, not death."

"You're not going to die."

"It's a street race!"

"I'm the best driver you've ever been in a car with."

I scoff, even though he's probably right.

"When I said distraction, I didn't mean this." I gesture to the line of fast, sleek, stupidly expensive sports cars. And the throng of sexy women sitting on the hoods, chatting up the drivers, just being racy. See what I did there?

"Promise it will work though."

I blow out an exhale, an unexpected thrill licking low in my stomach. I'm about to do something illegal. A street race!

I guess if we got caught I could always pretend Lorenzo kidnapped me.

"What's going on in that head of yours?"

"Nothing."

"In or out, Mia?"

"In."

"That's my girl. Let's do this."

Is it dumb that my heart rate ticks up when he calls me his girl?

Glancing at the beautiful women swarming around his car I decide that it's not dumb at all.

What's dumb is agreeing to sit shotgun for a street race.

———

THE REV of the engine wraps around me as my hands grip the strap of my seatbelt. Holy guacamole. I'm doing this.

"Ready, bellezza?"

"I think so."

Lorenzo's hand palms my thigh. "I got this, Mia. Trust me?"

Turning to him, his blue eyes bright, I nod. "I do."

"Good. We're up." He grins, tilting his head toward the starting line.

Lining up next to the car we're racing, Lorenzo murmurs to himself and focuses on the road, his face transforming as he commits to this dig.

A girl stands in between the cars, a red flag raised above her head. When she drops the flag, Lorenzo hits the accelerator and we jerk forward. My heart gallops in my chest, my palms breaking out in a sweat and who the hell even knows where my stomach is? Probably back at the starting line.

Lorenzo drives flawlessly, hugging curves and weaving through traffic effortlessly. Guiding us through tight spots, outmaneuvering red lights, he gains a solid lead on the other car.

When he blows past the finish line, I'm grinning like a lunatic, a high I've never experienced washing over me.

Lorenzo slows the car until we come to a complete stop.

Turning to me, his hand cradles my cheek, pulling me in for a hard kiss. "What did you think?"

"That was exhilarating!"

"You never cease to amaze me, Mia. I swear, the ride I'm taking with you beats the hell out of racing."

———

"I CAN'T BELIEVE you took this girl on a *Fast and Furious* experience." Lexi tosses a thumb in my direction while raising her eyebrows at Lorenzo.

"Ah, next time, she's going to drive." he grins, setting down two cappuccinos. "Are you girls really here to study?"

"Nope. Mia is here to see you and I'm here to enjoy the other sights." Lexi dips her head toward the table of men seated behind us.

Lorenzo snorts. "Let me know if you need an introduction."

"I always knew I liked you." Lexi lifts her cappuccino. "Can I also have a tiramisu?"

"Of course. And for you, bellezza?" He asks, playing with the edges of my hair.

"I'm fine, thanks."

"You sure? You skipped lunch." Lexi points at me.

Lorenzo frowns. "Do you feel okay?"

"Yes, I'm fine. Really." I pick up my cappuccino.

I gained four pounds since I've been in Rome. Four! The number is giving me serious anxiety and causing my fingers to twitch with the quickest solution to drop the weight.

But I'm trying to ignore the urge.

Trying so hard and Lexi and Lorenzo make it so much harder when they look at me like… the way they're looking at me now.

I sip my beverage, ignoring them.

"Enzo, your sister's on the phone." Simona, the hostess, steps onto the patio.

Lorenzo nods, tugging on my hair. "Let me know if you change your mind."

"I will, thanks."

Once he turns back into the restaurant, Lexi leans forward. "Don't even tell me your dieting while living in Rome. That's like masochistic as fuck."

Rolling my eyes, I change the subject until Simona drops off Lexi's tiramisu.

"You're cute together." She says to me, swaying next to our table.

"Uh, thanks." I smile. I don't really know Simona, but she seems nice.

"You must be pretty special; Enzo doesn't usually keep a girl around this long."

"Harsh." Lexi mutters, narrowing her gaze at Simona.

"I'm just telling her the truth." Simona shrugs, her eyes narrowing. "I wish someone told me before I slept with him." She adds, her voice sweet, her words jarring.

Then she spins around to check on another table.

"She's lying." Lexi grabs my wrist until I look at her. "She's jealous and trying to make you question your relationship with Lorenzo. Don't let her get in your head, girl."

"I won't." I say but the words fall flat.

Because all I can think about is the four pounds.

And how incredibly thin Simona is compared to me.

# 14

## LORENZO

"Enzo." Claudia's voice rings out as soon as I pick up the phone.

"What's going on?"

A sob travels through the line.

"Claudia, is Mama okay?"

"Enzo, come home."

"What's going on?" I repeat, already ripping off my apron and grabbing my car keys.

"Zio Benito." She takes a deep breath. "He … He's inherited all of Papa's shares for all of the companies. He's inherited all of the properties, the vineyards, everything. He's on the board! Benito is controlling Papa's legacy."

A string of curse words erupts from my mouth as ice flows through my veins.

All sounds cease except the pounding in my ears, the thrum of blood in my temples. Inhaling sharply, my hands begin to tremble.

"We have nothing." My sister whispers.

"I'm on my way." I hang up. "Simona, I need to go. Call

one of the girls to come in and help you. I'll pay you girls double for today."

Without waiting for a response, I leave the restaurant and drive home, barely seeing the other cars on the road, not bothering to stop at red lights.

"Lorenzo." Mama stands from the kitchen table as I barrel into our home. She isn't startled by my entrance or surprised to see me. The emerald ring on her finger shakes when she breathes.

"Is it true?"

"It's true."

"How bad?"

She averts her gaze, stepping out of my embrace.

"Mama, how bad?"

"We have nothing. Nothing except this home. And Angelina's."

"Why didn't you tell me? All this time, you knew?"

"I didn't want you to worry."

"Mama!"

"I should have confided in you and Claudia earlier. I thought … I don't know what I thought. I thought I could handle it, fix everything. But now it's too late." She holds her arms out wide. "We have lost everything." Then she drops her head to my chest and sobs.

Tears soak through the front of my shirt as I hug Mama, surprised by how fragile she feels in my arms.

Moments from the past year rush back. Me, swiping my credit card at every VIP booth without a second thought, crashing my Maserati, shopping in Firenze.

What the hell was I thinking?

Disappointment blazes through me and I hang my head. I've blown a lot of my earnings from the F1 circuit, never budgeted or thought about where my money was coming from.

And now, I don't have any.

Not enough to support Mama and Claudia with the life-style they are accustomed to living.

The weight of providing for my family, ensuring their security, guaranteeing their happiness, settles on my shoulders and takes root in my chest.

---

*MIA: Hey, all okay?*

Shit! Mia. I left her at Angelina's without even saying good-bye.

*Me: Mia, I'm sorry. Some things came up with my family and I had to leave.*

*Mia: Are you okay?*

*Me: Not sure yet.*

*Mia: Need a distraction?*

*Me: It's not a good time. I'll call you soon.*

---

TAKING another sip of the Negroni, I breathe in the orange scent, and try to calm my nerves. The Medusa head on my cufflink mocks me as I process Papa's lawyer and longtime friend, Rafaello's, words.

"Enzo, mi dispiace," he apologizes.

"I know."

Rafaello looks around, his eyes assessing. We're in the back of an old bar I've never been to, a place no one would recognize us. Rafaello is jumpy, a far cry from the usually collected, confident man I grew up calling zio.

He clears his throat, his fingers tapping against his glass. "He … Benito," he lowers his voice, "he got to your papa."

I narrow my gaze, silently imploring Rafaello to explain faster.

"He blackmailed him," he whispers, looking over his shoulder to make sure no one is listening.

My mind races over everything I know regarding Papa's business ventures, projects, and investments. I recall snippets from conversations and several documents I remember from his desk. Other than that, I don't know much. In fact, I'm embarrassed by how little I do know.

Silently cursing myself, I lean forward in my chair. "What did he have on Papa?"

Rafaello closes his eyes and a pained expression flits across his face. "I'm sorry, Lorenzo." Another apology.

"Rafaello, whatever you know, please just tell me. I need to fix this for Mama and Claudia."

He winces at the mention of Mama.

A trickle of dread spreads through my veins and I roll my shoulders forward, bracing myself for whatever is coming.

Rafaello takes a long sip of his Negroni and clears his throat again. "It was many years ago, you have to understand that. Your papa, he was different then, in a different place in his life."

"Just tell me."

"Salvatore, he met someone a long time ago, on one of his business trips. It was before Elenora, he would never do anything to hurt her."

I nod.

"Carmela was a fun and careless woman and after their weekend together, they kept in touch."

"And?"

"He would see her from time to time, mixing business

with pleasure, that kind of thing. Two months after your papa met Elenora, Carmela called him and told him that she was pregnant."

In the silence that follows, all the air from the bar disappears. I feel like I'm underwater, sinking, unable to draw oxygen into my lungs. I have a brother or another sister somewhere? Is Rafaello serious?

"Salvatore sent her money to help her with the pregnancy, medical bills, vitamins, those kinds of things. And afterward, well ... he helped support her and her son ever since."

A brother. I have a brother.

Panic grips me as I realize what this means. There is someone else who can claim Papa's wealth. Someone else who can manipulate the situation to rip away Mama's security. The eldest Barca male, the rightful heir to the Barca legacy, to the inheritance.

I breathe in sharply as the pieces click into place. Gulping my Negroni, I hiss as the Campari hits the back of my throat.

Rafaello knocks his knuckles against the table, looking away.

"So, Carmela, has she contacted you? Is that how Benito found out?"

"No, Benito knew all along. Right from the beginning. You have to remember how close Salvatore and Benito were; they were truly brothers, Lorenzo. Benito always knew about Carmela. He even helped set up the bank account that would ensure Anthony's future."

Anthony. My brother.

"Carmela died in a car accident four years ago. By then, Anthony was already of age. He had full access to his trust, so it seemed pointless to change anything. Benito had set everything up in a way where Anthony never knew who his father was, where the money was coming from, and Carmela preferred it that way. She was scared that Anthony would want to know his father, would want to come to Italy, and would leave her. He's all she had, and she wanted to keep it that way."

"Wait a minute," I raise my hand up to halt Rafaello's story, "Carmela and Anthony … they're not in Italy?"

"No. Carmela, she was an American. Anthony was born there. He lives in New York. In Brooklyn."

Pinching the bridge of my nose, I screw my eyes closed. "Then what happened?"

Rafaello leans back in his chair, more relaxed now that the secret is out.

"Carmela raised Anthony with your papa's money. The account was in Carmela's name with Anthony as a beneficiary, so after her passing he inherited everything and is in pretty good shape, financially speaking."

I nod, twirling my finger to hurry up and get to the part that matters.

"Once Salvatore was diagnosed, Benito started showing up. Playing the concerned brother role, wanting to mend fences. Salvatore never believed him. When his niceties didn't earn him a way in, Benito resorted to typical Benito behavior. He told Salvatore that if he didn't change his will to include him and to give him a role on the board, he would tell Elenora about Carmela. And Anthony."

I sit up in my chair so fast I give myself a head rush. "Mama doesn't know?"

Rafaello shakes his head.

"Why? Why didn't he tell her? He told her everything!" If there was ever a marriage to emulate, it was my parents'. I've never questioned my papa's loyalty to Mama nor her love for him. Until now.

*How could he not tell her he had another child?*

*A son.*

"The timing. Salvatore had just started dating Elenora when Carmela contacted him. He didn't want to push her away and risk losing her. Things were different back then. Not like today, with young couples living together before they marry. Hell, before they're even engaged." He takes a sip of his drink, flicking his hand. "Anyway, then Salvatore and Elenora married and he didn't want to ruin the honeymoon period of their marriage. Once you came along, he figured what was the point? He knew Carmela would never be an interference; she had more than enough money to live however she wished, she had sole custody of Anthony, and she didn't have to leave America. It was a win-win, so your papa never felt the need to share it with Elenora and upset her. Once Benito began to blackmail him, well, he didn't want his last days with Elenora to be filled with shame and guilt. He wanted to love her the way he always did. He hoped that by signing over everything to Benito, Elenora would never find out the truth. You have to understand, Benito promised he would take care of Elenora and you and Claudia the way Salvatore did. He swore to Salvatore that being the beneficiary wouldn't disrupt or interfere with your lifestyles."

"He lied."

"Of course he did. I never trusted Benito, not even when we were schoolchildren. But, by then, it was too late. Salvatore was grasping onto whatever he could still control. He refused to listen to reason because he didn't want anything to affect your mama and their last days together. So he chose to believe Benito. And maybe," Rafaello sighs, draining his Negroni, "maybe he really did believe Benito at that point. They were brothers after all."

Rafaello's explanation shifts memories from my childhood, scattered moments that stream through my consciousness, into perspective. If only Papa was here to explain it all.

"Now what?" I ask Rafaello.

"Now, Lorenzo, it's up to you. Whatever you do with this information, well, it's your decision. I have to get going." He extends his hand to me.

"Thank you, Rafaello. Thank you for telling me the truth."

"I hope it was the right thing to do."

"It was."

"We'll see. Good luck to you, Enzo." He reaches over and ruffles my hair like he did when I was a boy. "I'll see you around."

I nod and watch as Rafaello leaves the bar.

Then I order another Negroni.

## 15

## MIA

"Hey, girl, hey." Lexi sticks her head around my bedroom door.

"Hi."

"Whatcha doin'?"

"Just emailing my dad. We're going to FaceTime this weekend." I close my laptop.

She walks in my room, holding up a bottle of wine. Clad in a pair of leggings with a long, oversized sweater and boots, her green eyes glitter. "Wine time?"

"It's 1:00PM."

"And 5:00PM somewhere." She winks. "Come on. You've already done your school stuff for the day. Let's have some fun!" She tosses a pair of jeans at me. "Get dressed. We need to cross 'drinking at a public fountain' off our Rome bucket list. Especially before it's too cold for us to enjoy it."

She tucks the bottle into her shoulder bag and stares at me.

I roll my eyes but slide into the jeans. Tugging on my boots, I admit, "I could use the wine."

"No word from Enzo?"

"No, nothing since he messaged he'd call me soon. What's soon anyway?"

"I don't know girl, but for him to leave Angelina's without saying good-bye to you means it's serious. He's probably super preoccupied with family."

"Probably."

"Wine will help."

"Lead me to a public fountain."

---

LEXI WAS RIGHT; wine helps.

The frosty bite of not-winter stings my cheeks as Lexi and I sit under a fountain in Trastevere. It's late afternoon and the sun is sinking behind the centuries old, charming church in front of us. We finished the wine a while ago but the warmth from the strong, bold red still coats our bellies as we people watch.

Students with backpacks and shoulder bags walk home, their hands fumbling to send text messages and make plans for the evening. Old men with graying hair and knotty canes take slow steps, their hands tucked into the crooks of their wives' arms. The old women all wear their hair pulled back; wool shawls wrapped around their frail shoulders. An entire city swirls around us, bold and bright and beautiful.

"What happened with Pietro?" I ask Lexi.

"We had dinner together a few nights ago."

"And?" I prompt her.

She cringes. "He's engaged."

"What?" I shriek, my eyes widening.

"I know, right? I had no idea. What a dick."

"Totally."

Lexi bumps her shoulder against mine. "He's going to call you."

"Lorenzo?"

"Do you have another sexy, F1 driver, who whispers sweet nothings in Italian to you?"

"Shut it." I snort. "Do you really think so?"

"I know so. He's dealing with family drama. Why are you being so insecure about this?"

I shrug.

"Spill it girl."

"Have you seen him? He's totally gorgeous."

"Uh, so are you!"

"And then, the other day when Simona said —"

"She's ratchet."

"You should have seen the girls when we did that street race. They were all so glamorous, so effortless, I —"

"Need to stop comparing yourself to all these other women. Mia, Lorenzo likes *you*. He chose *you*. I imagine he has a colorful past but it's not like he can change it. So, you either have to believe he's telling you the truth and all these other women are in his past and be okay with that, or you shouldn't date him. Because you're going to drive yourself nuts second-guessing everything."

Sighing, I nod. "I know."

"I'll cheer you up." She pulls a second bottle of wine from her shoulder bag.

"Are you kidding me?"

"This conversation is getting too heavy. Time to lighten the mood."

"It's too cold. Let's go to a bar instead."

Lexi grins, wrapping an arm around my shoulders in a hug. "Yes! I knew I would break you down. A bar it is."

I snort, standing and gathering up my purse. Lexi links

her arm with mine and we set off to the nearest bar, happy hour about to begin.

---

LYRICS TO BON JOVI'S *"Living on a Prayer,"* ring out and the crowd claps wildly, beer bottles held overhead in elation. Lexi jumps up on the bar, shaking her ass and encouraging more cheering from the crowd.

Tears from laughing so hard burn my eyes as I watch her. I clap along with the guys jostling me on either side, and she smiles at me, reaching down to offer me a hand.

"No way."

She pulls harder as I resist. But then the guy behind me wraps his hands around my waist and gives me a boost up. Suddenly, I'm standing on a bar. On a freaking bar. Oh my God.

I look at Lexi in panic and she takes both of my hands in hers, tugging me closer. "Just dance," she yells over the noise of the bar.

The music changes, an Avicii song blaring from the speakers.

"Woo! I love this song," Lexi declares, her hair spilling forward as she raises her arms and shakes to the beat.

Laughing, I close my eyes and focus on the music, swirling my hips. Oh my God, I think I just flipped my hair. I feel someone tug on the back of my jeans, just below my knee. Turning, I bend down as the bartender hands me a shot glass. He winks and throws back his own shot. Glancing at the tiny glass in my hand, Lexi slaps my ass. "Drink it!"

I do. The alcohol burns a trail of fire down my throat as the guys below us yell out declarations of love. Snorting, laughter bubbles out of me like a volcano. The bar grows louder. Hotter. The colors are brighter, the shots more frequent.

Another guy reaches up and wraps his hands around the backs of my thighs, pulling me forward until I fall off the bar and into his open arms. "Why don't you dance for me babe?" he asks, his Australian accent thick.

Lexi hops off the bar, linking her arm through mine and pulling me away. "Sorry, dude. Your accent is delicious and all, but tonight is girls' night."

She winks at him and drags me to a makeshift dance floor. Lexi pulls me through the gyrating bodies, the laughter, the strong stench of hard liquor until we're in the center of the floor. Then we dance, sweat running down my back, my hair sticking to my neck. Our laughter mingles, eyes closed to the music.

If I could freeze a moment in time, tuck it away to pull out every now and then and remember how I feel right this second, it would be this one.

---

IT'S LATE when Lexi and I collapse into our beds. Tipsy from wine and vodka shots, buzzing with adrenaline from dancing, I send Lorenzo a message.

*Me: I miss you.*

It's four in the morning when my phone chimes with a response. Snatching my glasses off my bedside table, I glance at my phone, instantly awake.

Lorenzo.

Now he messages me?

*Lorenzo: What can you tell me about Brooklyn, NY?*
*Me: I'm not sure where you're going with this ...*
*Lorenzo: Long story. Sorry to bother you so late.*

*Me: All OK?*

Seconds stretch into minutes. I snuggle against my pillows and check my messages and email. Three missed FaceTime calls from Maura? I sit up again. Is she okay? It's strange for her to call several times in a row. I'm about to call her back when Lorenzo messages again.

*Lorenzo: Not really. Can't sleep. What are you doing awake so early?*

*Me: Is that a real question? I've been worried about you.*

*Lorenzo: I know. I'm sorry.*

*Me: ...*

*Lorenzo: I need you, Mia. Want to get breakfast?*

*Me: Okay.*

*Lorenzo: I'll pick you up in 15.*

Jeez, nothing like getting ready in a hurry. It's like hanging out with Lexi.

*Me: See you soon.*

Climbing out of bed, I tug on a pair of skinny jeans and the brown leather boots with the chunky heel that Emma tossed in my suitcase. She was right; they are super comfy. I pull on a thick cream sweater, brush my teeth, and pop in my contacts. Twenty minutes later, I walk out the front door and slide into the sleek leather seat of a red sports car.

"Buon giorno."

"Lorenzo, are you okay?"

He shakes his head. "I meant to get in touch with you sooner. There's been so much going on and I, God, I'm glad to see you, bellezza."

Placing a palm on his cheek, I lean forward. Lorenzo meets me halfway. His kiss is hard, as if he's trying to prove something to himself.

*But what is it?*

Pulling away, I study him, a coldness seeping through my body.

The skin under his eyes is bruised from lack of sleep. His hair is messy and sticks out in various directions, as if he's been pulling at it. Still, he looks sexy as hell. Effortlessly so. His white T-shirt pulls taut against his chest, stubble lining his jaw. A casual zip-up hoodie hugs his shoulders and ripped, designer jeans mold to his legs. He exudes confidence, a kind of assertiveness that is as attractive as it is menacing.

"Lorenzo." I whisper.

A shadow of a smile hugs his lips. "Be with me, Mia."

"Of course."

The engine of the car revs loudly. "Buckle up."

I barely click my seatbelt when Lorenzo releases the break and pulls out of the parking spot. The car lurches forward and Rome flies by outside my window.

Forty minutes pass before we turn off the Autostrade and drive for another five minutes in silence. Finally, Lorenzo makes a left turn, and we disappear down a narrow, winding road into a thick forest.

The sun peeks through the trees, light filtering through thick branches and dancing off colorful leaves. Reds and yellows and oranges glimmer. The land opens up into a clearing, the trees spaced out, and I learn that we are on a cliff, driving along the coast. The ocean shines before us, white foam dancing along the crests of curling waves. The sea beats dangerously against the jagged cliff rocks, spraying water and salt high into the air. Lorenzo turns right, his car hugging the road.

"It's beautiful." I gesture toward the water with my hand

"Isn't it?" he asks, his voice gruff, his eyes trained on mine.

"What's going on, Lorenzo?"

"You like waffles?"

"Um, what?"

"Waffles," he repeats, his gaze straying from the road again. "Do you like them?"

"Sure." I say, my fingers combing through the ends of my hair.

Oh God. How am I supposed to eat waffles? This is why I like Italian breakfasts. They're like air compared to an American morning meal. I look out the window again. My nerves heighten, a wave of panic rising in my chest.

*What if I tell him I'm developing a gluten allergy? Yes! I'm not eating gluten for two weeks to test myself. I can say that, can't I? Totally believable.*

"Great. The place we're going, it's the best. An American couple owns it. They moved out here a few years ago and opened up this tiny breakfast bar that specializes in American breakfast foods, but their waffles are most popular. I think you'll like it. A little taste of home."

My heart squeezes at his thoughtfulness and so many of the insecurities I've been struggling against for the past two days evaporate. "That sounds great."

His hand reaches over and laces with mine. "I'm glad you're here, Mia."

"Me too."

# 16

# LORENZO

I let Mia off the hook of ordering waffles if she promises to try a bite of mine. She agrees and orders a large coffee and two scrambled egg whites with a side of sautéed mushrooms.

Weird. I've never met an American who eats as healthy as she does. Must be the dancing.

I order a Belgian waffle and a side of bacon.

We grin at each other across the table as the server/hostess/cook/owner disappears into the kitchen. I love this place. It's a hidden gem that not many know about, especially not the tourists that flock to Italy each summer. But, those tourists add a lot of revenue to Angelina's, my family's only source of income for the foreseeable future. Sighing, I cross my arms on the table.

"Want to talk about it?" Mia offers, extending her hand to rest on my forearm.

"It's my family. I didn't mean to blow you off at Angelina's."

"I know, don't worry. I'm sorry things are sucking for you

right now." She wrinkles her nose. Her lips pout in thought, and I want to lean across the table and capture her mouth with mine.

"I found out on Monday that I have a brother I didn't know about. His name is Anthony."

Her eyes widen, her eyebrows disappearing into her hairline. "Oh, wow." Her fingers grip my skin.

"Yeah," I fight back a wave of laughter. "Oh."

"I don't know what I thought you were going to say, but that wasn't it. Are you okay?"

"I think so." After my late-night Facebook stalking—hell, if that didn't make me sound like every girl I never liked—it seems that Anthony Casale is a decent guy. He owns a microbrewery in Brooklyn. Now *that* was something I didn't expect. The heir to the Barca legacy making beer for a living.

"Does he happen to live in Brooklyn?"

"He does."

"That's cool. You know, this breakfast spot, the vibe and atmosphere, it's all very Brooklyn."

Chuckling, I lean forward and kiss my girl.

Mia grins, wrapping both hands around her mug. "You know, it's pretty cool you have another brother. I miss my mom so much; I would love to have a surprise sibling pop up. Just to have someone else in the world that could connect me to her."

"I never thought of it like that. Did you really dislike being an only child? I used to wish my parents never had Claudia."

"Trust me, being an only sucks. Regardless of your relationship with your sister, you always know that you can count on her. Even if it's only to confirm your parents are nuts or something, she'll always know and understand you in a way that no one, not even your closest friends, can. You have a special connection forever.

My friends all have siblings and even though they fight sometimes, especially Emma and her sisters, they're always there for each other. Lila would do anything for her brother Brandon; he's always looking out for her. Maura is a shadow of herself, barely existing, since she lost her twin, Adrian. That connection, if you're lucky enough to have it, you get to keep it for life. I always wanted that."

I nod, considering her words. "Yeah, I get what you're saying. And you're right." I cut my waffles. "It's funny, really. Since Papa passed, Claudia and I have grown so much closer. I see all these things in her that I never noticed before. And I wonder, was she always this considerate toward me and I never cared to pay attention before? Or is our relationship changing because of the situation we're facing?"

"Does it matter?"

"No, I guess not."

"So, what are you going to do about Anthony? Do you want to contact him?"

"I don't know," I admit. "I guess I'll have to talk to Claudia about it and see what she's most comfortable with."

Mia raises her eyebrows at me.

Smirking, I hold up my hands. "Okay, you're right about siblings. I couldn't imagine dealing with this without Claudia. Even though I still have to tell her about Anthony."

"You'll find the right words."

"Hope so."

We eat in silence for a few moments. Mia barely eats a third of her eggs before she places her fork and knife down.

"Not hungry?" I ask.

"It's still early."

"True. I did wake you when it was still dark out."

"It was worth it."

"Want to see something?"

"With you? Always."

---

"Wow." It falls from her mouth on a breath of air.

Sitting in the dip of a clearing, high above the waking towns below, the scene is beautiful. People, tiny like ants, shuffle to start their days. I picture them sweeping their front porches, sipping their espressos at kitchen tables, their eyes running along the lines of a newspaper. Life awakens around us. And here we sit, observing it all.

In the other direction, the ocean stretches until it meets the sky, a thin line marking the horizon. The sun beats down, warming the tops of our heads as icy tendrils of almost-winter lick at our cheeks from the strong wind.

"This is incredible." Mia pulls out her phone, snapping photos of the view. "Smile, Lorenzo."

Grinning, I hold her close, tucking her against my chest and wrapping my arms around her. Mia's frame feels tiny, almost fragile, in my arms. Scooping her closer, she shivers. I breathe in the scent of her hair, vanilla and something I can't place. Something uniquely Mia.

I didn't plan on coming here. I guess life surprises you sometimes, giving you something you didn't realize you needed. Back when I was a kid, this spot, on top of the world, made everything else inconsequential. Breathing in the cold air, holding it in my lungs, brings clarity to my mind. Exhaling, resolve shifts through me, building in my veins; I can do this. Even knowing Papa's deceit, Benito's manipulation, Anthony's existence, I can handle this.

And I want to.

I want to make things better for Mama, easier for Claudia, and protect Papa's legacy.

Grinning into Mia's thick brown hair, I kiss the back of her head. Being in her presence simplifies things or maybe she just makes me feel invincible.

# 17

## MIA

W hen I open my eyes in the morning, Lexi is sitting on the edge of my bed staring at me.

I jump. "Hi."

"Good morning, Petunia."

"You know it's creepy to watch people sleep, right?"

She rolls her eyes. "I wasn't staring at you. Just figuring out the nicest way to wake you. You should be grateful you woke up before I decided on an evil plan." She steeples her hands together, tapping her fingertips like an evil mastermind.

"How was your night with the hottie?"

"Banging." She smirks, twirling a thick piece of blond hair around her finger.

I choke on my laughter.

"The more important question is what's going on with you and Lorenzo? Tell me everything."

"We're good. We hung out yesterday and you were right, he does have a lot going on with his family."

"See?"

I nod.

"So, are you free tonight?"

"Why?"

"Why do you sound so skeptical? Can't I just hang out with my roomie?"

"Why Lexi?"

"Go to the Tre Fratelli concert with me. Please!"

"Okay."

"Wait, really?" Lexi narrows her gaze.

"Yes. It'll be fun."

"Oh my God. Who are you?"

Rolling my eyes, I grab a towel and clean clothes from my closet. "I'm going to shower."

"And then we'll discuss outfits for tonight."

"Something warm."

"Duh!"

---

*Lorenzo: Ciao bellezza, what are you doing tonight?*

*Me: I promised Lexi I'd go to a concert with her.*

*Lorenzo: Tre Fratelli?*

*Me: How'd you know?*

*Lorenzo: It's a pretty big deal.*

*Me: Oh. Want to come?*

*Lorenzo: You have no idea how badly but I'm going to tell Claudia tonight.*

*Me: Good luck!*

*Lorenzo: Message me once you're home?*

*Me: Of course. XO*

---

LEXI TUGS MY HAND, guiding me through throngs of students until we're closer to the stage. The grassy hill is swarming with people and littered with empty beer bottles and cigarette butts. The band is perched on top of the hill, the music floating down over the crowd. Students sway drunkenly to the beat, bottles raised over their heads.

It's positively freezing outside, and I'm grateful for the winter coat I wore over my wool scarf and knit sweater. I pull the cuffs down over my gloved fingers, and Lexi turns back to make sure I'm keeping pace with her. "I see some people from my art history class over here." She nods in the direction of her classmates.

"Okay." I follow her through the crowd until we arrive by her friends. I grin when I see a familiar face among the group. It's Pete, from my Italian Literature class.

"Hey, Mia." Pete throws an arm around my shoulder in greeting. "Want a beer?" He kicks a cooler that someone in the group must have brought along.

"Sure."

Pete grabs two beers, pops off the tops, and hands them to Lexi and me. "Cheers."

"Salute," Lexi addresses the group, raising the bottle above her head.

"Salute," a chorus of voices rings out.

Rolling my eyes, I take a swig of the beer.

"Not a beer drinker?" Pete guesses.

"Am I that obvious? I thought I kept a straight face."

Pete chuckles. "Nah, you totally grimaced."

"I really only like Blue Moon."

"With the oranges?"

"Exactly."

Pete laughs again.

Lexi loses herself in the crowd. Within minutes I spot her sitting atop some guy's shoulders, her beer bottle raised in the air, her jacket zipped up to her chin. She cheers on the band loudly.

"Your friend is hysterical." Pete comments.

"Tell me about it."

"How do you like the Literature class?"

"Yeah, I like it. I'm learning a lot from the readings. You?"

"It's okay. To be honest, I'm really behind."

"Too much traveling?"

"And partying." Pete pulls his hat lower on his head.

"Both acceptable reasons." I try my beer again, wincing.

"Tell that to my parents." Pete pulls a flask from his pocket. "Here, try this. You may like it better than beer."

"You came prepared." I take a sip. Liquid trickles down my throat, blazing a trail straight to my stomach. I sputter, covering my mouth with the back of my hand, as my eyes water.

"It's Scotch, straight from Scotland. Be careful, it sneaks up on you."

Between the music, the bite in the air, the jostling crowd, and Lexi's wild whooping, I drink more Scotch than I intend to.

After Tre Fratelli's second set, Lexi is kissing a guy I've never seen, and Pete bumps his shoulder against mine. "Want to see something cool?"

"Um, sure."

"It's this way." Pete leads me to the entrance to the park. "Through here."

He nods with his chin to an alleyway. The moonlight shifts, casting a shadow over his face. His eyes dart around for a moment and I realize we're alone.

Silence envelops us and I shiver. Pete tugs me closer into

his side, wrapping his arm around my middle. "Come," he whispers pulling me into the alleyway.

We walk in silence for several minutes before turning right. And then, the most beautiful thing happens. Right before my eyes, it's as if Ancient Rome unfolds. Pillars and stones and beautiful carvings that recount timeless stories etched all along the ruins.

"Wow," I whisper.

Pete tightens his grip on me. "I know, right?"

"This is amazing."

"This is Rome."

I nod, stepping out of Pete's grasp. I can imagine these temples and arches before they fell into ruin, before the empire collapsed. Inhaling, I see the senators walking the streets proudly in their robes. The beautiful women with dark curly hair, quick eyes, and soft smiles. The vestal virgins dressed in white. I hear the loud squawks of children playing in the streets, smell the sticky heat, the stench of animals. I detect the tinge of ferocious power and certain inevitability of a glorious time. A frozen moment.

Stepping forward, my boot catches on a rock and I jolt forward.

"Easy there." Pete catches me, his hand gripping my hip.

"Thanks." Taking a quick photo, I send it to the girls. "Oh my God. It's almost 2:00AM."

"Do you have a curfew or something?"

"No, I just, I didn't realize it was so late."

"We can hang for a bit."

Biting the corner of my mouth, I shake my head. "I think I should get back. I want to find Lexi."

"Lexi took off with that dude."

"Oh. Well, I should check in with her."

"What are you, her keeper? Relax, babe."

Babe? Is he kidding me?

"Thanks for showing me this, Pete." I gesture toward the ruins. "It's incredible. But I need to go."

Except Pete blocks my path, his hands gripping my waist, his mouth descending toward mine.

Turning my head, I push him away. "What is wrong with you?"

"Not even a goodnight kiss?" He sneers, pulling me closer. "Come on babe."

Shoving against his chest, I manage to push him back a few steps. "Don't touch me." I blurt out, nerves prickling my body, adrenaline spiking.

Pete laughs. "Take it easy, babe."

"I'm leaving now." I step around him, vibrating with awareness.

Behind me, Pete murmurs a stream of curses, followed by other words. Terrible words. Words that scrape across my skin and pick at old scabs.

"Damn prude. Who cares? Nothing but a fat bitch."

*Fat. Fat. Fat.*

I hustle out into the park, relief flooding me once I'm back among a group of people. Safety in numbers.

Spotting Lexi, she gestures that she's heading out with the guy she met.

I wave to her, turning to the exit.

Around me, students cheer and drink, couples kiss, friends laugh.

But all I can think about are Pete's words.

*Fat. Fat. Fat.*

They play in my head on an endless loop.

And cause big, fat tears to track my cheeks.

# 18

## LORENZO

S hit!

Hot espresso coats my tongue, burning my throat when I swallow.

10:00PM.

I should be out with Mia, or Sandro, but I can't keep delaying the conversation I need to have with Claudia, so here I am, sitting at the kitchen table hoping she comes home.

The minutes tick by slowly. I shuffle back and forth in front of the large windows that overlook our garden. Darkness surrounds the house, a gloomy fog and the chill of winter wrapping around the brown leaves. She'll be home soon, won't she? I can't carry this burden around for one more night. I've reached my limit; Claudia and Mama need to learn about Anthony.

"Enzo?" Claudia gasps, pressing a hand to the base of her throat. "You scared me! What are you doing here?"

"I live here." I grin, tipping my head to the kitchen table. "Want an espresso?"

"Now? It's so late." Claudia removes her coat and sets it

on the back of the chair. Two red love bites glare from the side of her neck. "We won't be able to sleep."

"I don't think we're going to sleep any time soon. Who marked your neck?"

Her head snaps up, her hand automatically covering the marks. "Is Mama okay?"

"Yes."

"I'll have tea."

"Who were you out with?"

Claudia shrugs, "Don't worry; it's nothing serious."

Placing the kettle on the stove, I turn to rest my back against the counter and cross my ankles. "Well, now I'm curious. And worried." I raise my eyebrows.

Tears collect in the corners of my sister's eyes and something in my chest cracks. *What stronzo is making her cry?* "Claudia?" I soften my tone. "Are you okay?"

Nodding, she dabs at her eyes, attempting a smile. "Don't worry about me. I'm fine. I can only deal with one issue at a time anyway so tell me why you're lurking in the kitchen drinking espresso so late at night?"

"Chamomile or peach?"

"Chamomile. Enzo?"

Bringing our beverages over to the table, I slide into the seat across from Claudia. I stare at her, stealing the seconds before I change her life forever.

*We have a brother.*

The words are on the tip of my tongue, but I don't tell her yet. She looks so worried, concern in the tightness of her lips, empathy in her eyes.

*Was she always so sincere?*

*Have I always overlooked her kindness, her compassion, for others?*

"Enzo? What is it?"

Sighing, I run my hand along my jaw. This is it. Time to tell her the truth. My leg bounces underneath the table and I'm grateful Claudia doesn't detect my nervousness.

*Just tell her.*

"Enzo?" Her voice is small, worry thick in her tone. "Is it Mama?"

*Tell her the truth.*

"We have a brother." I blurt out and immediately curse myself for being so careless as shock locks down Claudia's features.

"What?" she asks slowly as if she's speaking to a child. "What are you talking about?"

*Start at the beginning.*

Reaching across the table, I clasp Claudia's hand. "I went to see Rafaello."

"When?"

"This week."

"What did he say?"

"We have a brother…" I begin.

"That snake!" Is Claudia's first reaction when I finish relaying the information I received from Rafaello.

Holding my breath, I'm unsure if she means Papa, Benito, Rafaello, or our long-lost brother, Anthony. Maybe all of them?

"I can't believe he's Papa's brother."

My breath slowly escapes. She meant Benito.

"I know."

A tear trickles down Claudia's cheek, and she swats it away. "I can't believe this; I can't believe Papa would do this. Lie to Mama all these years. Put her in this position. What was he thinking?"

"I don't know."

"I'm so, ugh, I don't even know, angry. I'm angry and

then I feel guilty about being mad at my papa who's not even here to defend himself." Another tear rolls down her cheek. She closes her eyes, her fingertips massaging the center of her forehead.

"Don't feel guilty; I'm furious."

"We have to tell Mama."

"Tell me what?" Mama asks, waltzing into the kitchen, her eyebrows raised.

My breath catches in my throat and I cough but Claudia doesn't miss a beat.

"Mama, sit down. Let me prepare you some tea. Enzo and I would like to speak with you."

I turn my head so quickly, my neck cracks.

"What is it?" Mama asks, sitting down.

Claudia places a mug of tea in front of Mama and sits down next to me. Taking my hand underneath the table, she squeezes, calming my nerves. Her hand taps against my knee, forcing my bouncing leg to still.

"Lorenzo and I have recently learned that we have a brother in America."

Mama's face falls.

———

12:35AM

*Me: Hey Bellezza. How was the concert?*

1:08AM

*Me: Mia, do you and Lexi need a ride anywhere?*

1:47AM

*Me: Did you get home okay?*

2:05AM

*Me: Bella, I'm worried. Please let me know you're okay.*

"Hey." Claudia knocks on my bedroom door.

"Hey."

"Everything okay?" she nods toward my phone.

"Yeah." I shake my head. "I don't know. It's Mia, I can't get in touch with her."

"Mia, huh?" Claudia sits on the edge of my bed. "What's her story?"

"Story? She's an American exchange student. She's beautiful, soulful, super smart. She loves to read Dante and Petrarca's sonnets. She used to dance but now she's just, figuring things out for herself."

My sister narrows her gaze, studying me.

"What?"

"I never thought I'd see the day."

"What day?"

"You're falling in love with her."

I snort, shaking my head. "Nah, she's just, different."

"You have feelings for her." Claudia tosses a pillow at my head, grinning.

"Of course I have feelings for her; I'm dating her."

"Oh my God! You are?"

Dropping my head back, I pinch my nose. "Yes, and I don't brand her neck with marks. Who's the guy?"

"I came here to talk about Benito."

Snorting, I shake my head. "Of course you did."

"I have an idea."

Raising my eyebrows, I gesture for Claudia to continue.

"We need to get Benito's attention. We need to do something to draw him out for a confrontation. Right now, he's off the grid. We don't know where he is or how to contact him. No one does. If we don't let him know we're on to him, we could be waiting around for years while he drains millions of dollars from Papa's companies. He needs to know that we're going to contest Papa's will, even if it ends up in court for years. He can't get away with this and the sooner we take action, the better."

"Wow, Claud. When did you get so smart?"

"Oh, please. I've always been the smarter, better-looking Barca. You just never noticed because you're so self-absorbed."

I wince. She's right.

Claudia's eyes widen when I don't retaliate. "Enzo, I'm joking!"

"You're right, though."

"What is wrong with you? I'm really just joking. When did you get so sensitive?"

"Since all of this happened." I gesture around the room to indicate nearly losing our home.

She punches my arm. "Well, stop it. I liked you better when you were sharp and sarcastic. I don't know what to do with nice and considerate Enzo."

"Any ideas on how to get Benito's attention?"

"I'm still thinking on that part." Claudia sighs.

Thinking over several scenarios, the safest, most logical answer is to have him come to us. "I may know a way."

*But would it work?*

"Feel free to share your evil plan."

"Liguria."

"What about it?"

"I'll go up to the house and throw a party."

Chewing the corner of her mouth, Claudia nods. "So you'll access Benito's property, meaning he'll either contact you to tell you the house is no longer ours or he'll know that you're doing it to piss him off and get a rise out of him. Either way, he'll come around. And we can tell him that we know what he's up to and we're not going to let him get away with it."

"Exactly."

"That's brilliant."

"Glad you think so, little sister."

"You mean, smarter sister."

"Yeah." I reach out and tug her hair. "Okay."

"Bring Mia. I want to meet her for real and not just see her sitting at Angelina's." Claudia's smile is sincere, her eyes curious.

"Okay."

"And, don't tell Mama."

"Definitely not."

Claudia grins. "Let the plotting begin. 'Night Enzo."

"Buona notte, Claudia."

Picking up my phone to call Mia, relief floods my chest when a text appears.

2:55AM

*Mia: Hey. Sorry, tonight was a shit show. Talk tomorrow?*

*Me: You okay?*

*Mia: I think so.*

What the hell does that mean?

*Me: Did something happen? Are you hurt?*

*Mia: No, I'm okay.*

*Me: Bellezza... where are you? I'll come get you.*

*Mia: It's okay. I'm walking home now.*

Walking home? It's 3AM!

*Me: Send me your location. I'm on my way.*

# 19

# MIA

Dragging the sleeves of my coat over my tear-stained face, I take deep breaths. I've been aimlessly wandering for hours, Pete's words playing in my mind.

Words blending with images.

Of the food I ate today.

Of the bulge around my waistline.

Of the thickness hugging my arms.

I used to be the epitome of graceful, long and thin and slender.

Ballerina Mia.

Now I'm fat.

*Fat. Fat. Fat.*

And I can't get past it. The transformation from Ballerina Mia to College Kid Mia has been positive in so many ways. I've learned so much, embraced new experiences, accepted various challenges. I moved to Rome, soaked up a new culture and language, danced on a bar.

But old habits die hard.

And measuring my worth by my body, by the number on

the scale, by the degree of hunger in my belly, still dictates my life and outlook.

Right now, both seem pretty shitty.

When a Maserati GranTurismo pulls up beside me and Lorenzo jumps out, I'm nearly frozen. Some from shock, mostly from cold.

*He's here. He really came to find me.*

"Bellezza, what's going on?" His hands grip mine and squeeze. "You're ice. Come." He jostles me into his car, buckling in my seatbelt.

Slipping into the driver's seat, he directs all of the heat to me. "Mia, what the hell happened? Are you okay? Are you hurt?"

"No, I'm fine." The words come out in between my chattering teeth.

"I'm taking you home." Lorenzo U-turns, heading toward his house.

Tired, cold, and overwhelmed, I drop my head back and watch as Rome blurs outside my window.

---

IT'S NEARLY daybreak when Lorenzo pulls through the gates to his home and parks his car.

"Wow." The word falls from my mouth as I gaze up at the impressive villa. Brick and stone, turrets and large windows, an expansive lawn, Lorenzo's home belongs in a movie. "Your home is beautiful."

"Thank you. Let's get you inside."

The moment I cross the threshold into Lorenzo's house, I'm greeted with warmth. The heat from fireplaces swirls through the foyer, wrapping me up in a hug that chafes against the cold coating my skin.

The villa is stately with an exceptional attention to detail. Artwork lines the walls, sculptures sit in various corners, intricate designs are carved into the molding of doorframes. The living room ceiling even boasts a fresco!

"This way." Lorenzo guides me up a grand staircase to his bedroom, kicking the door closed behind him.

His room is large and masculine. A king-sized dark leather platform bed sits in the center of the room. One wall holds a massive television with several gaming stations hooked up. There's a couch and a mini fridge. The other side contains a mahogany writing desk and chair with floor-to-ceiling bookshelves holding Italian and English versions of all the classics. Model cars are enclosed in glass cases, framed photographs of Lorenzo's family sit atop his dresser, an accumulation of racing trophies and ribbons on display.

Turning, Lorenzo stands behind me. Running his hands up my back, he tugs on the ends of my hair until I look up.

"Mia."

"I like your room."

"Why have you been crying?"

Wrinkling my nose, I admit. "It's stupid."

"It's not stupid if you're this upset."

Stepping out of his embrace, I back pedal to the edge of his bed and sink into the mattress. "I'm exhausted, Lorenzo. Can we talk about this tomorrow?"

Tilting his head to the side, he studies me. "Bellezza, please. Just let me know you're really okay."

At the concern shadowing his eyes, the dip in his voice, emotion bubbles inside and spills over again. Damn it. As moisture collects in the corners of my eyes, Lorenzo swears and kneels at my feet, pushing in between my thighs and wrapping his arms around my back.

"What happened at Tre Fratelli, Mia?"

"Do you think I'm fat?" I hate that I ask the question, abhor how desperate I am for him to tell me he thinks I'm beautiful. But the words are out in the world now, coloring the space between us with an awkwardness that causes all of my insecurities to flare to life.

I hate them too.

"Are you fucking serious?" Lorenzo asks, his hand scrubbing along his jaw. His blue eyes darken, a tsunami of fury churning in their depths. He stands from the floor, pulling me up with him. "That's the stupidest thing I ever heard. You're the most beautiful woman I know. You're perfect. Why would you even think that? And worse, why the hell would you believe some stronzo who said it to piss you off?"

The tears escape and horror washes over Lorenzo's face.

"Bellezza, please. Don't cry." He whispers, hooking a finger underneath my chin and lifting my face to meet his. "You don't really believe that, do you?" Brushing a kiss across my lips, he pulls back, searching my eyes for a confirmation I can't give him.

Letting loose with a stream of swear words, Lorenzo shakes his head. "You do." His eyes shutter closed.

"It's just that, with ballet," I sigh, pinching the space in between my eyes. "I don't know. I'm sorry."

"Don't apologize." Lorenzo opens his eyes, resolve sweeping through them. "I'm falling in love with you, Mia Petrella. Now let me show you how I see you. And one day, I pray you see what I do." He reaches up, framing my face with his hands. Gazing into my eyes for a long moment, his mouth captures mine, searing in its intensity, gentle in its caress.

Lorenzo's hands drop as he unzips my coat, pushing it off my shoulders until it falls to his bed. Then he tugs my sweater up and over my head, breaking our kiss momentarily, to fling it on the floor. Looking down at me clad in a bra and jeans, a wicked grin crosses his mouth. "I love these," he traces a cluster of beauty marks at the top of my ribcage with his thumb, "because they are unique." His hand travels up, squeezing my right breast and flicking down the cup of my bra. "And these, because they are the perfect size for my hand." He bends his head, pulling my breast into his mouth and twirling his tongue around my nipple.

Groaning, my head drops back, my legs feeling weak.

He unclasps my bra and it drops to the floor. Pressing me back so I'm lying on his bed, he reaches behind his head and pulls off his sweater.

I inhale, my eyes traveling upward from the waistband of his jeans. I drink in the way his muscles ripple when he moves, his abs winking at me as he hovers over my body, his forearms bearing his weight as he cages me in. I run my hand up the side of his body, my fingers gliding over the ink swirling up his ribcage. His broad shoulders bunch as he shifts his weight, and I bite the inside of my cheek to keep the sigh from falling from my mouth.

Flicking one of his pierced nipples, I raise my eyebrows.

"A dare in university."

"So you never back down from a challenge?"

"I never back down from anything." He drops his head, moving down my body and dipping his tongue into my belly button. His hands clench my hips as he peppers kisses along my waist, biting the top of my jeans to pop open the button. "I love your body, because it's strong from so many years of dedication to ballet." He slides down the zipper and tugs off my pants.

I'm panting, able to hear each inhale and exhale. My fingers grip at Lorenzo's bedspread, my eyes dropping closed. Sensations I've never experienced rock through me.

I've never been so exposed before, so vulnerable, and the experience is as thrilling as it is frightening.

Lorenzo's fingers hook around my underwear, dragging them to the side. "And this part of you, well, it's perfect because I'm the only man to do this." He lowers his mouth and I buck off the bed, my hands fisting his hair as he works me over, building me up until I implode.

"Do you have any idea what you do to me? How you make me feel?" he asks, pressing his erection against me.

I gasp, still riding a natural high, desperate for more.

Desperate for everything.

Holy shit. We're doing this.

I'm doing this.

# 20

# LORENZO

"Lorenzo." She braces her elbows on the bed, staring up at me.

Splayed out beneath me, Mia is breathtaking. The details of her naked form should be captured by an artist, painted, and hanging in a museum somewhere.

"Are you starting to understand how perfect you are to me?" I ask, kissing her neck, rolling her until she's straddling me, pressing me into the mattress.

She leans forward, her lips shadowing mine, her ass rubbing against my erection, and I groan into her mouth. Wrapping my arms around her, my left forearm anchors across her back and my right hand slides up her neck, my fingers getting lost in her hair.

I kiss her tenderly, sweetly. At least, I try to. But the way her hips slowly move, the way she rocks against me, spurs me on. Before I can stop myself, I flip Mia over, laying her down beneath me once more. Covering her body with mine, lacing our fingers together, I pin her arms overhead.

Her eyes widen, heat exploding in their depths like firecrackers.

She licks her bottom lip seductively and my brain short-circuits.

I want to take her, right here, right now.

"Bellezza, tell me what you want." I bite down on her earlobe, loving the sounds that fall from her mouth.

"You. This. Show me Lorenzo, please, show me everything."

Pulling back, my eyes search hers, looking for any flicker of hesitancy.

Vulnerability swims in her eyes, black as midnight, but so does trust.

"Are you sure?"

"Yes."

"Mi amore." I brush the hair back from her face, capturing her lips again.

"Please." She murmurs against my mouth, her hands splayed along my back, her body arching into mine.

Reaching into my nightstand drawer, I pull out a condom and roll it on. Settling over her, I kiss her forehead, her eyelids, her nose, her lips. "Are you positive?"

"I trust you, Lorenzo."

"I love you, Mia." I say the words I've never said before as I rock into her.

Working her over slowly, I pay attention to every sound that falls from her lips, each twist of her body. Tracing her skin with my fingers, covering her body with my mouth, I take my time savoring every second of being with Mia.

And I fall so completely in love with my definition of perfection.

───────

THANK God I have the day off from Angelina's.

After everything that happened last night, I'm relieved Mama doesn't disturb me this morning, with Mia wrapped in my arms, naked in my bed.

We sleep in, the day already half over, when Mia turns to face me, the tip of her nose touching mine.

"Buon giorno, bellezza."

She grins, stretching slowly. "Good morning."

"How do you feel?"

"Amazing."

I chuckle, palming the swell of her ass. "How amazing?"

"The most amazing I've ever felt. In. My. Life."

"You're going to ruin me."

"Nah, after last night, I'm going to keep you."

I bark out a laugh, dropping my head to her shoulder.

Mia's hands find my cheeks and guide my face upwards until my eyes latch onto hers. Deep with awareness, dark with emotion, she presses her lips to mine.

"I love you more."

THE NEXT TWO weeks pass in a blur.

There is so much to prepare for the party Claudia and I are throwing at the Liguria house that each day is filled with obligations. My mornings are dedicated to party planning and preparation, my afternoons and evenings to Angelina's, and my nights, to my sweet Mia.

I'm excited when she agrees to spend the weekend with me in Liguria. I'm happy she wants to meet Claudia and Sandro as much as I want to introduce her to them.

But right now, in the hours when everyone else is dreaming, I keep her for myself. Worshipping her body, savoring her kiss, loving her completely.

NOVEMBER

# 21

# MIA

"You, the perpetual virgin." Maura hiccups. "You had sex?"

"I'm having sex. As in, for the past several weeks."

"Seriously?"

"You don't have to sound so incredulous about it." I huff, peeved at her less than enthusiastic reaction.

I should have called Lila or Emma, but I knew Maura was the only person who would be awake at this hour in the U.S. and I wanted to confide in at least one of my friends before I go away with Lorenzo for the weekend.

"Yes I do! Oh my God. I can't believe you would take the college pact so literal. You really jumped way out of your comfort zone."

"Thank you. I think."

"Are you okay? Was it okay? I thought you were waiting until … well, I'm not sure what you were waiting for, but did it go the way you hoped?"

I smile, my fingertips pressing against my lips. I've been sleeping with Lorenzo for weeks now and each time is new and exciting. The way he brands my lips with his kiss, the feel of his hands gliding down my body.

When he pushed inside of me for the first time, I tensed with the sharp shock of pain, but it quickly receded to a dull ache, which transformed into a building pressure, erupting and cascading through me in waves.

It was beautiful and perfect and the most meaningful connection I've ever shared with a guy, so, "Yes," I answer Maura. "It was perfect. And I'm great. It was more than what I hoped for."

"Well then, congratulations, Mia. And welcome to the club."

Rolling my eyes, I'm relieved Maura doesn't ask for a graphic play by play the way Lila and Emma will. "We're going away this weekend."

"Where to?"

"His family has a summer home in Liguria."

"It's November."

"I know but it will be nice to get away for a few days." I can't wait to spend time with Lorenzo outside of our hectic schedules, the bustle of Rome. It will be nice to go away, relax, and chill.

"Mia?" Maura asks. "You still there?"

"Yeah, sorry."

"Daydreaming?"

"Remembering."

"Wow, Mia. You got it bad. I'm happy for you."

"Thanks. How's everything by you?"

Silence ticks by for several seconds before she breathes out. "Things are fine. I'm going to see if Lila is coming home for Thanksgiving. I think I'll go up and see her, you know, after everything."

"That's a good idea. She can really use the support. I'm sorry I'm so far away when —"

"Don't apologize. You're supposed to be living your best life and I'm really proud of you. I just hope the timing works out for Thanksgiving. I miss you girls and seeing Lila would be nice."

Seconds tick by.

"Maura, is everything okay?"

"Sure. Sorry, Mia, I have to get going." She brushes me off, per usual. "I am really happy for you though. Be safe. Use protection." She barks out a jagged laugh.

"Okay. I'll talk to you soon."

"Yeah. You too. Bye, Mia."

"'Bye." I hang up and lie back on my bed. When I get home, when we're all in the same time zone, I'm not going to let Maura off the hook so easily.

Snuggling into my pillows, my thighs clench together and soreness travels through my limbs. A delicious ache. I stretch my arms overhead, enjoying the exhilaration still pumping through my veins, the memory of Lorenzo's touch hot on my skin.

---

WHEN I STEP out of Lorenzo's car, the sky is gray and gloomy, threatening rain. The breeze picks up and cold wind skates across my face. Pulling my scarf tighter around my neck, I link my fingers with his as we walk a handful of streets to his home in Liguria.

"Seriously? Are all of your homes out of a magazine?" I ask as we walk up to a beautiful yellow house built on top of stones that extend into the sea. Arched windows and a tile roof give off a Mediterranean vibe. Although the trees are barren and the garden empty, I can imagine the home in spring and summertime, bursting with color.

"It's beautiful," I whisper. Studying the scenery, I take a mental picture, committing each detail to memory. The way the wind echoes as it flits through my hair, the smell of salt and sea and November, it's all too perfect to forget.

Lorenzo doesn't say anything, but I sense him. The scent of his cologne mixed with a hint of basil washes over me. Pressing his hand to the small of my back, he shifts my body to block the brunt of the wind.

"I'm glad you came with me." Lorenzo grins, guiding me to the front door.

He closes the door behind us, dropping his keys into a marble bowl on a console. Lifting our travel bags higher, he flips his chin toward a grand staircase.

"I'm going to bring our stuff upstairs. Make yourself at home."

Walking slowly into the living room, I run my fingertips over the plush furniture and pause in front of several paintings. Frescoes are painted on the ceiling, the bookshelves lined with books in Italian, English, French, and German.

It's like being in a museum. Lorenzo's family owns a museum.

Sure, I went to private school in New York City. My dad earns a healthy living, and I've never wanted for anything. But this, Lorenzo's home, his car, his lifestyle, is on a whole other level than anything I've ever experienced.

Two leather chairs sit facing a gigantic window that takes up the entire back wall. It overlooks the sea; white foam sprays, leaving drops of salt on the glass. It's mesmerizing. I walk to the window, placing my fingertips against the cool glass and stare as the sea rolls in and recedes.

"Like the view?"

I turn and my breath catches in my throat. Lorenzo stands in the doorway, his right forearm bracing the weight of his body against the doorframe.

"It's incredible."

He nods once, pushing off the doorframe and walking toward me. His light gray sweater hugs his arms and his ripped jeans drag slightly on the ground now that he has traded his shoes for a pair of slippers. "What would you like to drink? Wine?"

"Sure." Sinking into a plush chair, I lean back and close my eyes.

In the background, I hear Lorenzo at the bar. The clink of glasses, the pop of a cork, the rattle of ice. I sense Lorenzo sink into the chair next to me. Opening my eyes, I roll my head to face him.

He hands me a glass of wine. "It's the one you liked best at the vineyard."

"Thank you."

"Salute." Lorenzo holds up his Negroni.

"Cheers." I take a sip of the wine, savoring it as it rolls over my tongue.

"Are you hungry?"

"No, I'm okay."

"Are you sure? You barely ate anything since we left Roma." He leans forward again, studying my face. "Do you feel okay?"

"Yes, I'm great, really."

"Okay, well I'll start dinner, and we can eat when you're hungry. I think you'll really like it."

"Can't wait." I grin but my chest tightens at his words.

What is he going to cook?

Ricotta and Grana Padano Gnocchi. You've got to be kidding me!

The aroma of homemade gnocchi and pesto sauce is delicious. The fresh basil is fragrant, and I breathe in deep, enjoying the scent as I set the dining table. Emma would be jumping up and down with pure happiness if any man—even an old and bald one—made her this meal. I feel like puking.

How am I going to get through this dinner? Of course Lorenzo will notice if I don't eat. Should I fake sick? No, he already asked me if I was feeling okay. Plus, I don't want to lie to the man I love.

*You already are.*

*Shut it!*

*Why couldn't he just make a salad?*

*Because you aren't rabbits*, Emma's voice echoes in my head.

"Mia," Lorenzo calls out. "Almost ready?"

"Yes," I say, laying the last utensil on the napkin.

"Take a seat." He enters the dining room carrying a big bowl of gnocchi.

I sit at my place setting and watch with dread as he lifts my plate. "Oh, that's more than enough," I say, placing my hand over my plate before he can drop another gigantic spoonful of carbs mixed with starch mixed with fat on top.

"You sure?" He frowns. "It's not a lot." He gestures to the bowl between us. My serving barely made a dent.

"It's perfect."

"Okay, would you like some vegetables?" He points to another plate of grilled vegetables.

"I'm good for now."

He spoons about three times as much gnocchi onto his plate, and I sigh in relief as I watch the gnocchi in the big bowl dwindle.

Lorenzo refills my wine glass and pours one for himself. "To the weekend."

"Thanks for inviting me, Lorenzo. This is pretty amazing. My friends will be super jealous when I tell them I had dinner at a private museum."

A shadow flickers across his face as his jawline tightens. "Buon appetito."

"Buon appetito," I reply, wishing he had a dog.

———

I EAT SEVEN GNOCCHI. Seven. I feel sick to my stomach, imagining the carbohydrates turning into cellulite on my thighs. Even if I could go back to dancing, it would be too late now that I've turned into a complete glutton, eating everything that passes under my nose.

"You didn't like it, did you?" Lorenzo asks, his eyes zeroing in on the leftover gnocchi on my plate.

"What? No, I loved it! I'm just full."

"Really?"

I make a cross over my heart. "Swear it. Thank you for cooking dinner."

"Of course. Wait until you see what I have for dessert."

"What?"

He chuckles, "It's for later." He drops his fork in his dish, his eyes darkening the longer he stares at me. "You sure you're done?"

"Positive."

"Come with me," he stands, extending his hand.

Clasping his fingers, I follow Lorenzo down a long hallway to a winding staircase.

"What is this?"

"You'll see."

# 22

## LORENZO

"Are you kidding me?"

I snort, watching Mia's expression as she takes in the indoor pool enclosed by stone walls and large windows. A tiny waterfall sits at one end, the water bubbling over the natural rocks.

"I love how easily impressed you are."

"This," she points to her face, "is seriously impressed. Your home is like being on vacation."

"Want to go in? The water's warm."

"Now?"

"Why not?" I pull my sweater over my head and raise my eyebrows.

Her eyes widen as she tracks my hands, watching as I unbutton the top of my jeans.

"Uh, I don't have a bathing suit."

"I've already seen you naked."

She blushes.

"And I'd love to see you naked right now."

Her cheeks flame.

Unzipping my jeans, they drop to my ankles before I step

out of them and kick them aside. Standing before Mia in my Armani boxer briefs, I watch her as he checks me out.

"Like what you see?" I tease her.

She snorts, rolling her eyes. "You're so arrogant."

"But you love it."

"Turn around." She twirls her finger.

"Are you joking?" My smile slips.

"Nope."

"But —"

"It's different watching someone undress under these harsh lights than it is in the dark when you're in the moment."

"Is that what this is about? I'll turn off the lights."

She snorts, exasperated. "Turn around."

"But I want to see you."

"If you listen, I'll let you feel me. Isn't that better?"

I turn around.

After several seconds, a splash sounds as she enters the pool.

I watch as she swims the length of the pool before diving in to catch her.

And when I do, I'm not letting go.

# 23

## MIA

Lorenzo's hands clasp my waist as he pulls closer, the water lapping between our chests. His eyes meet mine, dark blue, heated, and intense.

"No more running, Mia." He grins, capturing my mouth.

Moaning softly, I tilt my head to give him better access. He takes it greedily, slipping his tongue into my mouth. I shiver and feel him smile. His left hand frames my face as his right forearm anchors against my back, pressing me into him.

His kiss is tender; it consumes me until I'm drowning in him. Unable to think about anything other than the way his hands feel on my skin, the press of his lips against my neck, I wrap my legs around his waist. He chuckles, palming my ass and lifting me into his embrace.

Moving us to the edge of the pool, he cages me into the corner.

Lorenzo kisses me slowly, softly, reverently. I lose myself in his touch, in him. We float, locked in each other's embrace, until the bubbles from the waterfall swirl around us

Raking his teeth over his bottom lip, Lorenzo widens his eyes and I nod.

Being with him is like being drunk; he overwhelms all of my senses, fills me with courage, and encourages me to do things I've never done before, but want to. Badly.

I keep my eyes trained on his, nervous that if I blink, it will sever our connection, and I'll never get this moment back. Because in this moment, the heat in his eyes makes me feel beautiful in a way I never experienced before.

His hands are gentle as they shimmy my underwear down my legs. Hooking my legs around his torso, I close my eyes, the sound of the waterfall, of mine and Lorenzo's breath mingling, blocking out my nerves.

I focus on his touch, his kiss, the feel of him as he rocks into me, loving me underneath a waterfall in a goddamn museum.

---

"ENZO, WHERE ARE YOU?"

We're eating breakfast the next morning when Claudia arrives.

"Ciao! I'm so happy you're here." She grins when she spots me. Pulling me into a hug, she kisses both of my cheeks. "I've seen you at Angelina's of course but this is more official."

"It's good to meet you. I'm Mia."

"Oh, I know who you are. I've been dying to meet you. Mama too."

Lorenzo groans.

"We'll get ready for the party together." She turns to prepare an espresso.

Staring at her, I can't believe *she* wants to hang out with *me*.

Tall and slender, with long, black hair and dazzling green

eyes, Claudia is striking. She reminds me of the perfect ballerinas I used to watch when I was a little girl, still desperate to become Ballerina Mia.

Lorenzo quirks an eyebrow.

Clearing my throat, I say. "Sure, I'd love to."

"Okay, great. I've got some calls to make. I'll see you guys later." Claudia picks up her demitasse and exits the kitchen.

"Your sister is a model."

"Claudia? She's okay."

Snorting, I shake my head. "You're the worst."

"Bellezza, you know I'm the best."

---

THIS PARTY IS like the social event of the year.

For royalty.

Which, I'm starting to think Lorenzo and Claudia may be with how their guests clamor for their attention, seek out their time. While they're the perfect hosts, there's something detached in both of their demeanors, an aloofness I don't understand.

"Dance with me." Lorenzo draws me into his arms.

"Here?" I glance around at the cluster of women in designer dresses.

"Come on bellezza, you can dance circles around everyone here."

Grinning, I step into Lorenzo's embrace, close my eyes, and let the music guide me.

Cool air rides up my legs and underneath my dress as I twirl. Rich colors swirl like a kaleidoscope. My toes barely graze the ground as I dance in Lorenzo's arms. Turning in his arms, Lorenzo pulls me flush against his body. His arms wrap around my stomach, his fingers toying with mine. Settling his chin in the crook of my neck, he nips at my earlobe.

I shiver, laying my head back against his shoulder.

"You look happy," he whispers.

"I am happy."

"With me. Or because you're dancing?"

"Both."

"Good answer."

He turns me back toward him, his hands bracketing the sides of my face. "I want you to always be happy like this." He whispers, lowering his mouth to mine.

———

It's late when Lorenzo's friends begin to leave.

Or early, depending on your perception of time.

3:00AM.

Collapsing into a worn leather armchair, I survey the scene. Champagne flutes and crystal highball glasses litter the end tables and the top of the bar. The music has changed radically, now playing acoustic covers. Girls doze lazily on the armrests of armchairs, their men still lost in conversations, puffing on cigars and finishing their beverages.

I've never been to a house party like this before. It's a far cry from the handful of fraternity keggers Lila dragged me to. This party consists of flawless women in designer dresses with sharp eyes and soft smiles. Handsome men sporting cufflinks and loafers, their blazers adorned with colorful pocket squares. They kiss the necks of the beautiful girls and sip cocktails with assessing eyes and knowing smiles.

Lorenzo seemed different the entire evening, detached with everyone except his sister, his best friend Sandro, and me. While he welcomed everyone to his home, jumped behind the bar to concoct Negronis and Americanos when the bartender was tied up, and expertly cut cigars, the shadow only lifted from his eyes when we were dancing.

I noticed it with Claudia too. While we hung out this afternoon, she laughed, talked animatedly with her hands, and pranced in front of the mirror like a little girl playing dress-up. We sampled jewelry — she even lent me a ring and earrings for tonight — but among her friends, she acts sleek and sophisticated.

The vibe is strange, bordering on eerie. As if everyone here only socializes because their social spheres overlap and not because they really enjoy each other's company.

Sighing, my eyes grow heavy with sleep. Tucking my feet up, I snuggle into the armchair. My feet ache for the first time in months and it feels delicious, kind of like when your muscles hurt the first day back to the gym after New Year's Day.

I watch as Lorenzo and Claudia do the rounds with the remaining clusters of people. They offer guest bedrooms and call taxis. They nod politely and smile on cue. They are the personification of well-mannered, refined, aristocratic Europeans.

Meh, I'd rather sleep.

---

LORENZO MUST HAVE RELOCATED me during the night because it's nearly sunrise when I wake up in his bed. My stomach is rolling, my body like dead weight. Feeling full to the point of bursting, I know what will make me feel better, cleaner.

*A whole cannoli. You ate a whole cannoli.*

*Ew, Mia.*

*Lorenzo thinks you're beautiful.*

*But you're not. You're disgusting.*
*Don't do it. He likes you the way you are.*
*But do you like you the way you are?*
*He'll break up with you if you gain weight.*
*Fat. Fat. Fat.*
*Don't you want to sleep tonight?*

Groaning, I make my way to the bathroom, my head aching with all of my thoughts clamoring for attention. Closing the bathroom door, the fullness in my stomach aches and I'm desperate for the gnawing emptiness, the delicious light-headedness, the purity of being clean.

I know the second I do it, I'll be able to sleep soundly.

Pulling back my hair, I kneel in front of the toilet and lift the lid, wincing when it bangs against the back of the toilet, the noise jarring. I place my forehead in my hands and stare at the water in the bowl, glimpses of my reflection flickering in the darkness. Then, I press two fingers of my right hand to the back of my throat and heave.

# 24

## LORENZO

W hen I wake at night, the house is quiet. I keep my eyes closed, listening for Mia's soft breathing, her slight snore. But there's nothing. Reaching my hand out, the space next to me is empty, the sheet and comforter turned back into a neat triangle.

*Where is she?*

*Is she hungry?*

*Sick?*

*Does she need me?*

Slipping out of bed, I make my way down the hallway, when I hear a cough, followed by a choking sound.

*Mia's sick!*

*Why didn't she wake me?*

Stalking to the bathroom, I throw open the door and flip on the light.

Freezing, my chest tightens as I take in the scene before me. Confusion followed by a blaze of anger consumes me as Mia turns her head, flinching when her eyes meet mine.

Shame and guilt flicker across her face as disbelief rocks my system.

My Mia, with the fingers of her right hand disappearing down her throat, making herself gag and choke. My hand lashes out, yanking her upright and closing around her wrist as she drops her fingers from her mouth.

"What the hell are you doing?" I growl.

"Get out."

"Mia, what the fuck is this?" I gesture wildly around the bathroom.

"Lorenzo, please, just go."

"No! Answer me. Do you do this shit?" I shake her wrist in my hand.

She doesn't answer, doesn't even look up.

"Fuck!" I yell, dropping her wrist. My hands automatically curl into fists and I slam my right fist through the wall behind the toilet bowl. Pain radiates up my arm, my knuckles come away raw and bloody. Without looking at her, I turn around and leave the bathroom, flipping the light off.

# 25

# MIA

I suck in air sharply and it claws at my raw throat, burning with each inhale, stinging with every exhale.

*Oh my God.*

*Lorenzo saw me.*

*He saw everything.*

Disgust rolled off his body and radiated from his pores.

His disappointment hangs heavy in the air, suffocating me even though he's left the bathroom. Staring at the hole in the bathroom wall, I hang my head in shame.

Rinsing my mouth out at the faucet, I brush my teeth with my finger and some toothpaste I find. Walking back to the room, I hear Lorenzo banging around in the kitchen, probably preparing an espresso. Or a Negroni.

Pulling on an oversized sweater and a pair of boots, I pack my bag quickly and slip out the side entrance of the house.

The air is cold when it hits my face, the breeze chafing against my skin. Keeping my head down, I burrow my chin into the neck of my sweater. I left my coat hanging in the hall closet, but I'd rather freeze to death then face Lorenzo. I never want to see the disgust, the horror, the pure revulsion cross anyone's face like that again. Tears sting the corners of my eyes, and I blink to hold them in.

*Please don't fall, please don't fall.*

"Scusa." A deep voice says as I nearly walk into an elderly man.

"I'm sorry."

"Don't worry," he responds, his hands clutching my shoulders to steady himself.

I look up, stunned as I find myself face to face with Lorenzo …when he's seventy.

The man offers a smile, patting my shoulders in thanks. "Buona giornata."

"Have a good day," I repeat, turning my head to watch him walk down Lorenzo's street.

So strange.

Shaking my head, I focus on getting back to Rome.

Bursting into the train station, I'm relieved that the next train departs in seven minutes. I buy a ticket and duck into the nearest restroom to pull myself together.

Tears stain my cheeks as thoughts ricochet around my brain.

*How could he see me like that?*

*How could he ever want me now, knowing how weak I am?*

*Knowing my darkest secret?*

*He won't; it's over.*

Slipping onto the train, I walk to the back and close my eyes.

*Lorenzo: Mia? Where are you??*

*Lorenzo: Hello?? Where did you go?*

*Lorenzo: Please, just tell me you're okay. Please.*

*Lorenzo: Mia???*

# 26

## LORENZO

I'm grateful that Claudia is still sleeping when the front door opens. The relief I feel that Mia is back nearly chokes me. Anger still courses through my veins at what I saw in the bathroom.

*Why is she hurting herself?*

*Why didn't she tell me?*

*How do I help her?*

But right now, I just want to pull her into my arms, and comfort her.

I'm staring out the window, my arms braced on an antique table, so I don't see him come in. But when he clears his throat, the relief I feel evaporates like smoke.

"Benito," I say without turning around.

"Ah, nephew, so good to see you. Why didn't you invite me to last night's soiree?" His voice is low and gravelly after too many years of hard drinking and smoking.

I turn to face him, my eyes widening when I see how much he's aged. My papa's brother was always a handsome man, a natural charmer. How else can one get by on years of gambling, cheating, and whoring? But now he looks old, tired, and frail. "What are you doing here?"

"I think the question you should be answering is what are you doing here? This is no longer your home, Enzo; surely Rafaello passed along that knowledge when you met with him, hmm?"

*How the hell does he know I met with Rafaello?*

I keep my face impassive; he could be bluffing.

"Is that why that beautiful girl left here in tears?" he asks. "Did she find out that you're not actually worth all of this?" He holds his arms out, glancing around the massive room.

*When the hell did he see Mia?*

*Don't give him anything to use against you, Enzo.*

"I don't know what game you think you're playing, Benito, but you're not going to win. I don't know how you managed to change Papa's mind and sneak your way into his will, but I will not let you destroy what took him a lifetime to build. I will not let you destroy his legacy."

"Ah, Enzo, but there is nothing you can do about it. It's all quite clear. Please, tell Elenora to stop avoiding my calls. The sooner we sort out Salvatore's will, *his last wishes*, the easier it will be for her in the long term. Financially and in other areas."

"What does that mean?" *Damn it, don't take the bait!*

"You really know nothing, Enzo. Such a shame." He clucks his tongue. "Salvatore's son. You could have been something." He gestures to my frame. "Instead, he spoiled you, indulged you too much. Let you grow up into nothing but a boy who likes to race cars. And I hear you're not even good enough for that anymore."

I grit my teeth, biting down on my tongue until I taste blood. Metallic like rust. "I don't know what you're trying to prove but don't think you're going to drag my papa's reputation through the mud, taint his name with yours. Don't for one second think that I will let you hurt Mama and Claudia."

"Is that all?"

I remain silent.

"Well, at least Salvatore taught you how to hold your tongue, no?" Before he turns away he calls out, "Good morning, sleeping beauty. I know you're here so you may as well come out and kiss your uncle hello."

Claudia's frame shadows the doorway. "Uncle."

He turns, kissing her forehead. "As beautiful and radiant as ever, cara."

She looks at me over his shoulder, her face blank.

"Now, I really must be going, since it seems you're not going to invite me for an espresso."

Neither Claudia nor I say a word.

"So be it. Until next time." Benito waves his hand and places a hat on his head.

"And, Enzo, it really is chilly this morning. Next time you have a girlfriend leave you, the least you can do is make sure she is properly dressed."

Claudia's eyes widen. I glare at Benito.

He chuckles, clapping his hands together as he strolls out of the house, closing the door behind him.

I put my fist through another wall.

---

"WHERE DID SHE GO? WHAT HAPPENED?" Claudia asks me on the ride back to Roma.

"Don't want to talk about it."

"Oh, come on, Enzo. Maybe I can help."

"Doubtful."

Claudia huffs, crossing her arms over her chest, her brightly polished fingernails tapping in frustration.

"Fine." I slam the heel of my hand against the steering wheel. "I saw her." I pause. "She did something and I got angry, yelled at her a bit. She took off."

Thick, perfectly shaped eyebrows rise above her Versace frames. "Hence the hole in the bathroom wall."

I narrow my eyes at her and turn my attention back to the road.

"I'm sorry, Enzo. I really did like her. So who was it?"

"Who was what?"

"It's sweet that you're trying to protect her, even now, after everything."

"What are you talking about?"

"Which one of your friends did she bang?"

I brake so hard that both our necks strain against the seat-belts before slamming into the headrests. "What did you say?"

"Are you crazy? You scared the shit out of me!" Claudia yells, punching me in the arm.

"What did you say?"

"Who did she sleep with?"

"No one!" I roar. "That's what you thought? That my girlfr— that Mia hooked up with someone last night?"

Claudia pushes her sunglasses on top of her head, her eyes flashing. "What else did you see that got you so mad that you put your hand through a wall?"

I punch the steering wheel again, pain traveling up my arm from my knuckle on my ring finger. I think it's broken. "She … Mia … she was throwing up."

"You're angry because she drank too much and got sick?"

"What? No! She was making herself throw up, on

purpose." It comes out on an exhale, a secret leaked in the confines of the car.

"Jesu, Enzo, that's serious." Claudia murmurs, putting the pieces together. "She needs support, guidance. Not your temper. Do you have any idea how humiliated she must have felt for you to see her like that?"

Cursing myself, I grip the steering wheel tighter because I messed up.

"I know."

"What are you going to do about it?"

I shake my head.

"Enzo?"

"I don't know, Claudia."

Easing my foot off of the break, I pull back onto the road, and continue the drive to Roma.

# MIA

"We should talk." Words that no girl wants to hear.

I've been avoiding Lorenzo for over a week, ignoring his calls, not responding to his messages, giving up my study spot, even changing the route I take to school.

*How could I face him after everything he saw?*

And yet, here he is, standing outside the door of Paola and Gianluca's apartment.

"Look, I know you've been avoiding Angelina's."

*I should invite him in, shouldn't I?*

*You're not supposed to have these serious, life-altering conversations on a doorstep, are you?*

Lila would know exactly how to handle this situation. I should have talked to her, but then I would have to tell her everything. Lila and Emma and Maura.

*Oh God, what are they going to think of me?*

"Mia."

*Why is this so hard?*

*And excruciatingly embarrassing?*

*Why is this my life?*

"Can I come in?"

Pushing the door open, I step aside, waiting for Lorenzo to enter the apartment.

The atmosphere crackles and my throat dries, as if Lorenzo has sucked all the oxygen from the room. My cheeks are on fire, burning and blushing and sticky hot. My hands grow sweaty and clammy. I feel feverish.

"Mia?"

*Look up. Don't look up. Look up. Don't look up.*

I squeeze my eyes shut. I don't want to meet Lorenzo's eyes, or have him see straight to my soul; I don't want him to know all the ugly bits I hide there.

"Mia, look at me," Lorenzo brings his forehead down to rest against mine. "Mi amore, please."

But that word. Amore. Love.

I raise my head as his hands slide down my neck, my shoulders, my arms, until they clasp mine. He pulls my arms back with his, nestling our hands into the small of my back. Then he dips his head and kisses me.

Sweet and gentle.

Overflowing with compassion and understanding.

Forgiveness.

"We should talk."

"I know." I finally say.

Lorenzo's mouth is tight as he sits down on the couch, a tick working his jaw.

Perching on the edge of the couch, I'm ready to spring from the room and lock myself in the bathroom.

I think I'm going to be sick.

And this time, it won't even be on purpose.

I swallow. It's like pouring mud down a drain.

Lorenzo breathes out, running a hand along his jaw like he does when he's agitated. "Look, I'm not sure how to start this conversation. What I saw in Liguria, I've never seen anything like that before. Why Mia?" His voice is gentle, but I detect the undercurrent of frustration. "Why do you hurt yourself? I don't understand. You're beautiful. You're perfect. Why do you do that to yourself?"

I look away.

*Why do I do it?*

It's been for so long now.

The binging and purging, the hiding food, the avoiding food, the obsession with food.

Late nights reveling in the angry rumble and ferocious clawing deep in my stomach. Beautiful mornings of light-headed giddiness.

Pure, ethereal, exquisite emptiness.

Self-control. Discipline. Willpower.

Knowing I could rule my body and command my mind.

Secretly scrutinizing other dancers, noting the graceful bend of their bodies, like a willow tree in spring, as if a gentle breeze stirred them. Watching the elegant lines of their limbs, their flawless turnouts, the way they moved through the air, floating above the rest of us.

*I wanted that.*

I wanted it so badly; the desire to be perfect tasted better than chocolate ever could.

"Answer me, Mia." Lorenzo's voice is sharp, his patience waning. "Please, whatever you're thinking, just tell me."

"I wanted it too badly."

"Wanted what?"

"I wanted to be the perfect dancer. I wanted to fly across stages around the world and be so flawless that when you watched me, you wouldn't be able to tear your eyes away. Or blink." I meet his gaze, a spark igniting low in my stomach. "You don't understand."

"So help me understand. I want to understand." He's

exasperated now, his eyes pleading with me. "I'm sitting here, begging you to tell me, why the hell you do that when you're already all of those things! I can't tear my eyes from you; I am scared to blink when we're together for fear that I might miss something."

I shake my head, blinking to hold back the tears that sting behind my eyes. "I'm not. I'm not any of those things. I'm nothing now." I gesture toward my knee. "I'll never be anything worthy of all the effort, the time, the years of commitment. I dedicated my entire life to dance, to being the best, and now I have nothing to show for it except a hideous scar and thighs that rub together when I walk." I groan, embarrassed for letting that little truth slip out. "It's disgusting. I'm disgusting! How can you even stand to look at me? To kiss me?"

"Are you serious right now?" Lorenzo springs to his feet, his face beautiful in his outrage. His jaw strains in fury, the lines strong and fierce. If I wasn't so enamored by him, if I wasn't so humiliated, I would let myself be moved by the emotions radiating from him. "I am in love with you, Mia. I don't care what the scale says or if you have a second helping at dinner. I want you to be healthy and happy and right now, you're neither."

For a moment, I'm scared he's going to put his hand through another wall. His anger is palpable, rolling through the room like a storm cloud.

"Do you have any idea how badly I want you? I want it all, Mia." He closes his eyes as if in pain. "But you can't give me half of what I give you, can you?"

Forget about turning the tables on me, he straight up flips them over.

"What do you mean?"

"What do I mean? How can you give yourself to anyone?

Even a part of yourself? You're so wrapped up in your own head. Counting calories or bites or whatever the hell you do before running off to the bathroom and hurting yourself. Not telling anyone, not letting anyone in on your secret. You would never ask for help. How can I trust you, when you don't trust anyone? Tell me, do your friends from home know about this?"

The blood drains from my face, my skin paling.

"I didn't think so." He laughs, but its empty. "You're killing me right now because no matter how hard I try to be enough for you, you're too goddamn empty for anyone to fill up. You need to want to be whole before anyone else can come close to being enough."

He's staring at me, waiting for a reaction. A response. Something.

Those words, his wrath, the truth, rips into me with waves of pain so strong, I drown.

And my lifeline, the only thing I cling to, is the emptiness.

"You should go."

He covers his eyes with his hands. "Mia, please. I want to help you. I want to be with you. Let me in, bellezza. Let me help you. But you need to take the first step."

Silence hangs between us, the air heavy with awkwardness.

Lorenzo's face crumbles. Stalking to the door, he glances at me once over his shoulder, and then he's gone.

# 28

# LORENZO

M ia sits still as a statue, her face pale, her eyes blank. Somehow, she manages to look simultaneously stricken and peaceful.

Anger simmers in my veins, clouding my mind with questions I don't have the answers to.

*How can I help her?*

*Why doesn't she want help?*

*Can't she see she's hurting herself?*

Blinded by the intensity rocking through me, I nearly sideswipe Lexi as I barrel down the street toward my car.

"Whoa there, sailor. Where's the fire?"

Turning, her expression slips when she sees my face. "What's wrong? Is Mia okay?" she asks, concerned. And yet that concern is misplaced. She doesn't even know the real Mia.

Mia is a master of deception.

I laugh in response, the sound harsh. "Yeah. She's great." Sliding into my GranTurismo, I pull into the midday traffic.

As soon as I hit the Autostrade, I open her up, weaving in and out of cars, speeding by blaring horns and rude gestures.

Driving with the windows down, the cold air slaps me in the face like a sheet of ice water. My system cools, reason returns.

And in its wake, fear reigns.

Because my girl is hurting herself and I have no idea how to help her.

I don't know the first thing about being the man she needs me to be.

I wasn't messing around when I told her I want it all.

I still do; I want her.

But the image of her when I flipped on the light in the bathroom, stricken and desperate, is tattooed on my eyelids. The sound of her choking fills my throat with dread.

*How do you help someone who doesn't want to be helped?*

---

IT'S LATE when I park in the horseshoe driveway of Sandro's house. Knocking on the door, the housekeeper lets me in and gestures that Sandro is upstairs.

I knock twice on his bedroom door.

"Yeah?"

Stepping into his room, I'm greeted by the smell of tobacco and mint.

"Hey." I nod at Sandro and kick the door closed behind me.

"You look like shit. Want some tea?"

"No thanks."

"You sure? It's calming as hell."

"I'm good."

"I'm surprised you didn't stop by earlier. Claudia told me

things went south with Benito," he reaches into his desk drawer and tosses me a set of keys.

Shit. I forgot all about Benito while processing everything with Mia.

"Thanks for locking the house up." I was in such a hurry to find Mia that I left a set of keys on the table with a note.

"No problem." Sandro waves a hand at me. "I'm glad you confronted Benito but Enzo, he's going to fight you tooth and nail to ensure you don't contest your papa's will."

"I know."

"Still…shit with Benito is solvable. Why do you look like someone keyed your ride?"

"Got some other shit going on." I scrape a hand along my jaw.

"With Mia?"

"Yeah."

"She must be incredible in bed, no?"

"Don't say another word."

"Are you kidding me right now? You're not going to share the dirty details?"

"I'm serious, Sandro."

Sandro lets out a low whistle. "Damn. This one's got you whipped. Jesu, Enzo, we used to kick girls back and forth like passing a football."

"Mia's not some girl."

"Then you better figure out your shit and not let her go."

# 29

# MIA

W hen I open the door and step outside, the air bites at my cheeks, forcing me to pull my scarf up higher. Thick clouds hang over the city, casting a solemn feel amid the cobblestone streets and old-fashioned shutters.

It's officially winter.

Hoisting my backpack up higher on my shoulders, I pop in my earbuds, the throaty voices of The Avett Brothers poring through.

Walking over to Castel Sant'Angelo, I pause on the bridge, drinking in the view. A series of bridges cross back and forth over the Tiber River, like archways connecting the past and the future, the old and the new. Kicking at a stray pebble, I breathe in the cold, the scenery, the city.

Rome has changed me.

Raindrops fall from the sky, tiny, cold droplets of water dotting my hair and disappearing into my scarf. I have an umbrella in my backpack, but I'd rather stand in the rain and look at bridges, connect to this moment.

Breathe in this experience.

The growl of an engine envelops me.

I'd like to say I don't see him.

But who could miss a red Maserati on a cloudy, somber day in Rome?

When Lorenzo's car glides up next to me, I tug an earbud out of my ear and let it dangle from my shoulder. "I and Love and You" plays softly.

"Get in."

The rain picks up speed, pelting me with cold and wind and ice. Shivering, I tuck my chin into my scarf, pulling my fingertips up into the cuffs of my coat.

"I'm serious, Mia."

Seconds tick by. Strands of wet hair stick to my cheeks. Rainwater seeps past my scarf, down my neck, into my shirt.

The bright color of his car is out of place in this scene.

The water below churns furiously under the bridge.

The traffic around us ceases to exist.

Lorenzo's four-way flashers blink in the rain.

"Goddamn it, Mia. Get in the car." He steps out. A five o'clock shadow covers the lower half of his face, hiding his dimple. He's wearing dark jeans that sit low on his hips and a sweater that hugs his biceps, emphasizing his broad shoulders.

He stalks toward me, and I stare, mesmerized. His eyes flash up to mine in a warning, a threat, a promise.

Reaching out, he wraps his fingers around my wrist, pulling me into his arms. I breathe in his scent, spicy cologne, a hint of basil, and leather.

"Mia." It's a statement. He always says my name like it's the answer to a question instead of the question itself. His fingers weave through my hair, pushing the wet strands away from my face. "Look at me."

I do and I'm lost to him.

When he leans down, my breath hitches, but he doesn't

pause. He never pauses. He's probably never even looked at these bridges before.

His mouth captures mine, his lips moving slowly. Pulling back, he angles his head, looking at me hard. A growl escapes from his throat and he drags me forward, up on my toes. This time, he kisses me with abandon, hungrily and greedily, devouring the last of my resolve.

Melting into him, I meet him kiss for kiss, nip for nip. Our mouths grind together, desperate and passionate and frantic.

"Get in my car, Mia."

This time, breathless and trembling, I listen.

# 30

# LORENZO

I swear this girl is going to be the end of me.

When I see her standing on the Sant'Angelo Bridge, staring pensively out across the Tiber, in the pouring rain, I don't know whether to laugh and hug her, yell and shake her, or just kiss her senseless.

Her hair is wet, matted to her forehead, and she's visibly shaking from the cold. Yet she doesn't notice; she's lost to her thoughts. Her eyes drink in every move I make. They never leave my face and still, she says nothing. The rain keeps falling, cars drive by, and Mia stands before me. Her cheeks are red, her lips quiver, her eyes earnest.

Just seeing her causes my heart rate to spike and slow all at once.

I kiss her senseless.

---

WHEN I PARK in front of my house, I pull Mia out of the car, lift her in my arms, and carry her to my bedroom.

"You're freezing." I tug off her wet clothes, wrap her in a

blanket, and deposit her in the center of my bed. Crawling next to her, I push her hair out of her face.

"Mia."

A smile twitches over her lips.

Running my nose along her jawline, I breathe her in and plant kisses down the side of her neck.

"Why do you do it?"

She inhales sharply.

"Tell me," I prod again.

She burrows closer, dropping her face to my chest, her ear pressed against my heart.

"Can't hear you." I kiss the spot just below her ear.

She sighs and flops back, her hair splayed across my pillow. "I can't help it anymore. I know it's wrong, but I don't know how to stop."

Laying down next to her, I toss a leg over both of hers, my hand finding her hip.

"I need you to be straight with me. I don't know anything about this. But I'm here for you."

Her fingers pick at the blanket.

"How long?"

"What do you mean?"

I take a deep breath; she's going to fight me on every question. I wish I possessed patience, but there isn't a Barca on the planet with that type of understanding. "How long have you been starving yourself, or making yourself throw up, or just hating on food in general?"

She winces at the questions. "A long time."

"I need answers, cara. I can't help you if you're going to push me away."

"It started when I was eleven."

Eleven! I clench my hand into a fist and roll my head away from hers to check my anger. "Why?"

"After my mom died, I threw myself into dance. Every part of my life revolved around ballet; I always knew I wanted to be a ballerina. I used to watch the older girls, you know? There was one girl, Amy. She was perfect. When she danced, I couldn't tear my eyes away. It was as if she was a part of the music. I wanted to be just like her, dance like her. One day, the director of our program cut her. Apparently, she didn't have the right figure anymore. She was too curvy, too busty. Too big. I guess it had been going on for a while, her body changing, her gaining weight, but I never noticed until she was gone. I knew I never wanted that to be me, so I vowed to control my body so it wouldn't control my life, my future as a dancer. I started watching everything I ate, counting calories. And when it was too much, I would throw it back up, cleanse my system. After a while, I just felt better empty."

"Mia." My heart lodges in my throat. That is one of the saddest things I've ever heard. No little girl should carry a burden so big it dictates what she eats. All of my best and favorite family memories occurred around a meal, around a table. How did Mia miss out on all of that? "Didn't your father notice?"

"He was lost after my mom died. He tried; he really did do his best. And he thought it was great that I had dance, something to pour my energy into other than my mom's loss. What did he really know about raising a pre-teen girl on his own?" She lets the question dangle in the air between us. "Once he met Claire, he became caught up in her, her life, their romance."

"When did he marry Claire?"

"They started dating when I was fourteen, got engaged when I was fifteen, married when I was sixteen."

"And you don't like her?"

"She's okay. She's not like a terrible person or anything. She's just cold, detached. I guess I don't really know her; she's hard to warm up to. She never wanted kids, and I don't think she was thrilled to learn Dad had a teenager. By the time they married, I only had two years until college. Well, one and half. She liked to point that out." Mia laughs wryly. "She never took much of an interest in me. When Dad started traveling for work, Claire would tag along, and I was on my own. The whole thing, it wasn't as hard to hide as you'd think."

"What about your friends?"

"I was an expert by college. And it really isn't that crazy in the dance circle to be a bit obsessed about your weight." She shrugs. "A lot of the girls I danced with did similar things. It was never spoken of, but deep down, we all knew. And we all did it. So we all kept quiet. Like an unspoken agreement."

I run my thumb over her knuckles. Back and forth. "What do we do now?"

Her eyes widen, a tiny flicker of hope in their dark depths.

"I'm not going anywhere, Mia."

"Promise?"

"Swear it."

---

ANTHONY CASALE'S profile picture on Facebook stares back at me as I sit in front of my laptop, my knee bouncing up and down.

Mia is leaving next month. In six weeks, she'll be on a plane heading back to New York, to her life and her friends. And I don't want to let her go. Sandro is right; I need to figure out my shit.

Closing my eyes, I remember our first night together, the way her skin shuddered beneath my touch, the taste of her kiss, how she gripped me so tight I swore I saw Heaven.

I'm losing my grasp on reality as I lose myself in her.

Six weeks.

But can I follow Mia to another country? How could I do that to Mama and Claudia, especially now, with Benito hanging over our heads like a dark cloud? I can't go.

Can I?

Banging my fist on my desk, I watch as my laptop jumps several centimeters. I'm insane if I think this can work. It can't. I mean, it's too damn cliché. American study abroad student falls in love with Italian guy and they live happily ever after?

What a joke.

I log out of Facebook.

Leaving my room, I walk to the kitchen and pour myself a glass of water.

"You look very serious, Lorenzo," Mama comments.

"Mama." I jump at the sound of her voice, the contents of my glass sloshing over the rim.

Mama chuckles. "It all worked out with the girl, no?"

I sigh, rubbing a hand over my face. "Kind of."

"What does that mean?"

"Yes, it worked out. We're together."

Mama claps her hands. "Excellent. I would love to meet her. Should we do a dinner?"

"She's leaving. She goes back to America before Christmas."

"You know, Lorenzo, I happen to own a restaurant. I think I can manage having a dinner in the next month."

I snort, "I didn't mean about dinner. I mean she's leaving. As in, we aren't going to be together in six weeks." Are we?

"Why not?"

"She lives in America!" I sit down at the table.

"You've always wanted to go to America. To New York."

"I can't just leave Italy. Not now."

"Don't look at me like that, Lorenzo. There's no reason for you to stop living your life. Everything will be sorted. Besides, if she is the one, you would be a fool to let her go without trying to be together."

I open my mouth, but Mama raises her hand, silencing me.

"I'm not saying it's going to be easy, or without sacrifice, or without disappointments. But nothing real in life, especially relationships, is free of these challenges. If you love her, if you want to be with her, then you will." She shrugs. "And if you don't, you won't. But it's up to you and her. I've never known you to quit so easily before." She kisses my cheek to take the sting out of her words. "Don't give up on the things worth fighting for. I'm going to Angelina's now. I'll see you tonight."

"Okay. Ciao." I bounce up from the table, knocking my water glass over. Leaving it, I take the stairs two at a time and sit down at my desk.

Logging back into Facebook, I pull up Anthony Casale's profile.

*Don't give up on the things worth fighting for.*

Opening a private message, I begin to type.

# 31

## MIA

"Buona sera, bellezza." Lorenzo grins, walking toward my table at Angelina's.

"Ciao."

"Hungry for lunch?"

I nod slowly.

"I'll be right back."

Lorenzo has been helping me adjust to a healthy lifestyle. We both know it's not enough, and I agreed—promised—that I would seek out professional help once I'm home. But for now, he's doing everything he can to take care of me. And I'm doing everything I can to let him.

It's hard, especially at night. My mind recalls everything I consumed during the day, each bite, every single calorie. And it swells in my stomach, expanding into my throat, until I feel like I can't breathe. Purging was a part of my nightly ritual and old habits die hard.

I fight the urge to make myself throw up. I do ballet combinations around my room. Or stretch. Watch the clock. Pick up a book.

But Lorenzo is the best distraction.

And sex.

Which is why I've been spending nearly every night stretched out across his bed, underneath him, straddling him, snuggled against him.

"Here you go." He places a plate and bowl down in front of me. "A vegetable salad and minestrone soup, no pasta."

"Grazie."

"Prego." He sits down across from me as I test the soup. "It's hot."

Too late. Scalding the tip of my tongue, I place the spoon down on a napkin. "It's hot."

He pushes the salad forward. "Start with this."

Spearing an eggplant, zucchini, and a roasted red pepper onto my fork, I take a bite. "It's really good."

Lorenzo snags a red pepper from my dish and pops it into his mouth.

In exchange for my honesty, Lorenzo has declared himself my personal chef, creating well-balanced meals each day for lunch. And usually dinner. He sits with me while I eat to ensure I'm consuming my food.

I thought I would hate his meddling, being under the scrutiny of his observant eyes. But it's not like that; instead, he picks at my plate, or makes a plate for himself, and we hang out, eat lunch together.

I confide in him when I skip breakfast or throw up late at night. And even though pain flashes in his eyes at my confessions, I never see disappointment.

Day by day, my new normal becomes a little bit easier to manage.

---

"Mia." My dad's broad grin lights up my screen.

"Hi, Daddy."

"It's good to see you, sweetheart. How are you? The pictures you sent in your last email are incredible. How's Rome?"

"Everything is great. This city is amazing."

"Are you fluent yet?"

"I think so."

"Really?" His eyes widen. "Mia, that's wonderful. I'm so proud of you. Your mom would be incredibly proud of the woman you've become."

Tears dot my eyes, stinging as I hold them in. If only my dad knew the truth, knew about me hiding food and throwing up and lying. Would he still be proud of me? Would she?

"Thanks," I say, swallowing down the guilt. "What are you doing for Thanksgiving?"

"Oh, you know, the usual. It will be quiet this year without you. We'll miss you."

"I'll miss you too."

"What are your Thanksgiving plans? Still planning to celebrate?"

"Yeah. Paola and Gianluca are cooking a big feast for Lexi and me and some of our friends. It's really thoughtful of them. I think I'll make everyone go around the table and say one thing they're grateful for, just like Mom used to." We haven't done that since the year she passed, but somehow, surrounded by my transplant family in Italy, it feels like the right time to reinstate old customs.

"That sounds really special. I'm happy you're keeping up with old traditions. Mom always loved doing that."

When did we stop talking about her? And how are we bringing up memories from the past so easily now? Dad isn't upset or unwilling to talk about her. Was it always me making things strained?

"I want to ask you something."

After several beats of silence, Dad prompts, "What is it, Mia?"

"I met someone."

"Okay," Dad says slowly, probably trying to follow my train of thought.

"I want to invite him to New York for Christmas."

"Where is he from? What's his name? Will it be okay with his family for him to miss the holiday?"

"His name is Lorenzo. He's Italian. I'm not sure what his family will think. I wanted to check with you before I invite him."

"Is it serious?"

I nod.

Dad chuckles. "Your mom, she would really love this. You. Dating an Italian."

"You think?"

Dad nods. "Don't think you're off the hook Mia, I want the story on this guy. But you know you can always invite any of your friends, or boyfriends, home."

"Thanks Daddy."

"Sure. And, Mia?"

"Yeah."

"Maybe once you're home we can do dinner one night, just you and me?"

My heart feels heavy as I recognize the hope in Dad's voice. Did I hinder our relationship more than I realized?

"That would be great, Dad. I'd love to."

He smiles, the relief on his face increasing my guilt. "Great. Okay, let me know about Christmas."

"I will. Love you, Daddy."

"Love you more, Mia. Have a good night."

"'Bye."

Staring at my blank laptop screen, a wave of longing for home washes over me. When I go home, I will spend more time with Dad, give us the chance to get to know each other again. And that means trying more with Claire too.

Maybe you have to leave your comfort zone to understand the pieces of your life that are lacking, the parts you're most grateful for, and the future you want to pursue.

## 32

# LORENZO

"One green salad with chicken and a side of grilled vegetables." I place the plate in front of Mia.

"Grazie." She picks up her fork and dips the tines in olive oil before spearing a piece of chicken.

"How's your day going?"

"It's going. I want to ask you something."

"Good, because I want to ask you something too."

"Really?" she raises an eyebrow. The seriousness in her gaze unsettles me.

*Is something wrong?*

"You first, bellezza."

"Do you want to come home with me for Christmas?" she blurts out. "I mean, I completely understand if you can't, or you have your own family thing planned, or whatever, but —"

"That would be awesome." I place my hand over hers to halt her rambling. "I'd love to spend Christmas with you in New York, Mia."

She grins. "Really?"

"Absolutely. And, I'd like to invite you for dinner on

Saturday with my family. Mama's jealous since Claudia keeps going on and on about you. She's partly convinced I made you up since you sneak out of my house so early every morning."

Snorting, Mia grins. "I just didn't want your mom to get the wrong impression of me."

"So, you'd rather her think I made you up?"

She shrugs.

"Or that I'm with girls other than you?"

"Lorenzo!" Mia swats my arm and I tug her forward, pressing a kiss against her mouth.

"I'll pick you up at 7:00PM on Saturday."

"Okay."

"I need to get back to the kitchen."

"See you later tonight."

"You can stay for breakfast tomorrow."

"See you later tonight!"

---

MY HEAD IS ALREADY in New York.

Because I'm going to celebrate Christmas with Mia.

And I'm going to meet my brother.

Anthony's response on Facebook caught me off-guard. Not because he replied to my message, but because I wasn't prepared for his response.

*Anthony: Hey, man. Good to hear from you. I've been waiting for your message. It'd be good to chat. Are you free to FaceTime this weekend?*

Good to hear from you.

I've been waiting for your message.

What the hell does that mean? How long has he known about me? And who told me?

Who knows what's true anymore?

*Me: Hey, absolutely. Let me know what time works best for you.*

But first, I have to tell my sister.

"Claudia!" I shout when I enter the house.

"Is everything okay?" Claudia appears at the top of the stairs. "Is it Mama?"

"Come down, I have to tell you something."

"What's wrong?" Claudia walks down the stairs, concern shadowing her eyes. "I did something." I tell her about messaging Anthony.

"You messaged him on Facebook, and you didn't tell me?"

Sighing, I grab my sister's hand. "I wasn't trying to keep anything from you Claud, I swear. I didn't tell anyone. I didn't know if he would answer, and I didn't want to get your hopes up if nothing came of it. That's why I'm telling you now."

"What did he say?"

I tell her about the message. "It was only one message; I haven't talked to him yet or anything."

"Do you think I should be there? Does he even know about me?"

"I have no idea. I don't know what he knows."

*Good to hear from you.*

*I've been waiting for your message.*

"Okay, Claud, here's what I'm thinking. Let me talk to him for a few minutes and then bring you up and you can jump on FaceTime if he's open to it."

"Yeah. Okay. I want to meet him."

"I know what you mean."

PACING AROUND THE HOUSE, I glance at the clock at least once every five minutes. Driving myself crazy, I message Mia to see what she's eating for lunch. I know it's a little stalker-ish, but I can't help worrying about her.

Instead of texting me back, she calls. "A tuna salad."

"Protein. Good job."

"What are you doing today?"

"It's going to sound crazy, but I'm FaceTiming with Anthony."

"Your brother? Woah. How did that come about?"

I fill her in on the Facebook message.

"What? Why didn't you tell me?"

"Honestly, I didn't want to say anything before I knew if he would respond. And it didn't feel right telling anyone until I spoke to Claudia. I'm sorry, bellezza, I wasn't trying to keep anything from you."

Uncertainty swirls in my stomach at her silence.

"No, that makes sense. I understand. See what I meant about siblings?"

"Yes, you were right."

"I know you have a lot going on, Lorenzo. And I know you were angry with me for keeping my food issues from you. But you've also kept a lot from me. You never told me the purpose of the party in Liguria until afterwards. We have to be honest with each other if this is going to work."

Pinching the bridge of my nose, I nod. She's right.

"I know, amore. I promise, after I speak with Anthony, you'll be my first call."

"Duh."

"What?"

"Just call me."

Hanging up, I check the time.

Forty-two more minutes.

ANTHONY'S MOUTH curls from a firm, thin line into a sincere smile and time stops. For a moment, it's as if I am looking at a younger version of Papa. It's him, the way his left eyebrow slants over his eye, the shape of his mouth, the line of his jaw. Even if I was harboring any doubt that Anthony is my brother —and I'm not—I wouldn't have any uncertainty now.

"Hey, man. I'm Anthony. Good to connect with you. Thanks for taking the time to reach out," Anthony says, his New York accent strong.

"Ciao. It's nice to meet you. I'm Lorenzo."

"Yeah, give me twenty. I'm busy with something." Anthony turns away from the screen, yelling at someone over his shoulder. "Sounds good." He turns back to me. "Sorry about that. Our delivery is late today." He shrugs. "How you doin'? I'm glad you got in touch with me. I was hoping you would reach out. I'm really sorry for your loss." He bows his head respectfully, his shoulders straight. Like Papa's.

*Your loss. Your loss. Your loss.*

I guess he never was Papa's son, even though he looks just like him.

"Thanks. I appreciate it. Listen, I'm not sure how to go about this conversation. I'm glad you wrote me back and this," I gesture at the screen, signaling between us, "is cool. I don't know if you know, but I also have a sister and she—"

"Ah great, man. Where is Claudia? I'd love to meet her."

*What the hell is going on?*

*How does he know all about us when we know nothing about him?*

"Hi." Claudia waves, bouncing up from my desk chair and entering the frame. "It's nice to meet you."

"Pleasure's all mine. But listen guys, I don't have a lot of time, and I think it's important I tell you a few things."

"That'd be great." Claudia leans closer to the screen.

"Cool. So about a year ago, your dad reached out to me." He pauses, letting the information sink in as Claudia's mouth drops open. "Yeah." He nods, reading our expressions. "I was surprised too. Anyway, at that point, I was just getting everything started here at the brewery." He gestures behind him where a few taps are set up and visible on screen. "I really thought the whole thing was a massive joke, but Salvatore insisted we meet so he came to New York."

Papa's last business trip. I remember the trip well even though I was in Bologna at the time. Mama was worried, but Papa assured her that this was important to ensure his legacy. Well, that makes a lot more sense now.

"Okay," Claudia says slowly. "What happened?"

"Salvatore and I went out for dinner. There's real good Italian food here, the legit shit, you know?"

We nod, even though Italy obviously has the best Italian food in the world.

"Yeah, so we go out to dinner and Salvatore tells me all this shit. How he met my mom, how they hooked up, how he was already seeing your mom when he found out about me. He apologized about never taking an active role in my life. But I'm not angry or anything, you know, about not having a dad growing up. Though it would have been cool as hell to grow up with you guys." He shrugs.

"I thanked him for supporting my mom and me all these years because there's no way we could have our lifestyle on a kindergarten teacher's salary. We talked for a bit about our lives, Italy, the future. And then he tells me that he's dying I didn't know what to say. I almost wanted to laugh, you know? Like, why tell me now you're my dad if you're just going to leave? But then, he shows me a picture of you guys." Anthony shakes his head. "You're a lot older now than you are in your photo, Claudia."

Claudia laughs. "Was I eating a gelato? Papa always carried that photo around. Remember?" She looks at me.

I nod, recalling the photo instantly, remembering the day well. We were vacationing for the month in Santa Margherita Ligure. That was the trip that spurred Papa to buy the Liguria home for Mama. It had been a hot and sticky day; we spent it running in and out of the ocean. A few of the boys I ran around with and I tried to spy into the cabanas of the girls we knew, see if we could catch them naked. Papa bought us huge gelato cones, and Claudia dove into hers, strawberry and lemon dripping down her chubby cheeks.

"Yeah," Anthony confirms, "you had ice cream all over your face." He chuckles. "So yeah, then Salvatore tells me all about this beef with your uncle Benito, things from the past. He tells me that he wants to spend the rest of his time with your mom, making her happy, enjoying whatever they have left." He sighs, rubbing his hand along his jaw.

Claudia elbows me in the ribs. "You do that."

"I know. Listen." I nod toward the screen.

Anthony continues. "And I can respect that. I mean, it's pretty incredible how much he loves your mom, even after all those years together. I tell him that and he laughs, throws his arm around my shoulders and thanks me. I said, 'for what?' And he hands me an envelope. He says that inside is his will, the future of his businesses, his legacy."

"I had no idea what to make of any of it. But he asked me to hold on to it. He explained that this will mentions a previous will he filed in Italy so it shouldn't present any legal issues when Benito contests it. Salvatore said that there would come a time when you, Lorenzo," he looks at me, "would reach out to me. He said he didn't know if it would be in kindness or in rage." Anthony chuckles again. "I guess we both have his temper, huh? Anyway, he said you would contact me and when you did, that's when it would be time."

"Time for what?" I ask.

"Time to open it." He holds up a large envelope, showing Claudia and me Papa's seal, thick red wax with a wolf stamped in the center.

Forever a Roman.

Claudia breathes out. "You didn't open it?" She gestures toward the unbroken seal.

Anthony's eyes cut to her. "Of course not. We're family."

*We're family. We're family. We're family.*

Jesu.

I guess we are.

"Thank you." Claudia says with so much sincerity, she tears up.

Anthony looks at me.

"You ready to open it?"

He picks up a knife and breaks through the seal, opening the envelope. A stack of papers and several smaller envelopes slide out. "These are for you guys." He holds up two of the smaller envelopes. "And there's one for your mom. And one for me." He grins, setting them aside. Then, his eyes scan over the front page of the will. They widen in shock as he begins to read.

And my heart fucking stops.

# 33

## MIA

"He left you half his … his everything?" I throw my hands up, unsure what everything entails, but knowing it's a lot. Like a whole lot. Sitting down on the edge of my bed, I watch as Lorenzo paces in front of me.

To the door, turn. To the window, turn.

Lorenzo shakes his head, plopping down next to me and scooting backwards until his back rests against the headboard. "No, not half. He has all his businesses, all his holdings, his companies, investments, etc. He left half to Mama, and half to be divided three ways between me, Claudia, and Anthony."

I let out a low whistle. "Damn."

"Yeah. And, he left me the Liguria home."

"Are you kidding me?"

Lorenzo shakes his head, watching me closely. "Well, not yet. It's supposed to be a wedding present."

"Wow, your dad must really have wanted a daughter-in-law."

Lorenzo snickers. "Yeah. You."

Rolling my eyes, I ask "What are you going to do now?"

"What do you mean?"

"You could do anything. I mean, you studied business, right? Or you could pursue racing. What's next for you?" I inquire. I know he doesn't want to work at Angelina's forever.

"Oh, about that." He rolls onto his stomach, pulling me down next to him.

"Yes, about that."

He rests his hand on my hip and throws a leg over mine, tugging me closer. "How do you feel about me coming to New York on a more permanent basis?"

"Shut up! Are you serious?"

"Yes. I want to come and spend Christmas with you in New York and then stay there. You only have one more semester at school and the commute between Philadelphia and New York is a hell of a lot easier than Philadelphia to Rome."

"Only two hours."

"Exactly. And it gives me a chance to get to know my brother. Anthony offered me a job."

"As a brewer? Aren't you more of a wine person?"

"Yeah, but Claudia got the vineyards."

My mouth falls open again and Lorenzo laughs. "That was a joke."

"Really? How am I supposed to know? You're the only family I know who owns vineyards." I swat his arm.

"Not as a brewer. To help him expand the business."

"Oh. That makes a lot of sense."

"But, I think it will only be a side gig because I want to race again."

"Really?" I grin.

"Really. And, there is the United States Grand Prix so…"

"You're really coming to New York?"

"I'm really coming wherever you are."

My heart beats faster at his words.

God, the things this man does to me.

Leaning up, I press my mouth against his, my hands sliding down his back. Lorenzo rolls on top of me, kissing me hard, sucking my bottom lip in between his teeth.

My eyes close as he scatters kisses along my jawline, down my neck. I start to work his shirt up his abdomen when he pulls back, grabbing my ass one last time.

"Uh-uh. We have to go."

"What? Now?"

"Unless you want to be late to my mama's dinner."

"No way." I scramble out from underneath him. "I just need fifteen minutes, okay?"

"For what?"

I gesture toward my leggings and Converse sneakers. I can hear Emma yelling, Lila scoffing, and Maura laughing all the way from the U.S. "I'm not meeting your mother looking like this."

"You look beautiful."

"Just give me ten, okay?"

He flops back against my pillows. "As long as I can watch."

Rolling my eyes, I dig into my closet for something to wear.

Oh, who am I kidding? Lexi and I already decided on my outfit last night.

And Emma approved it via message this morning.

* * *

"YOUR HOME IS BEAUTIFUL. Thank you for inviting me to

dinner." I smile at Lorenzo's mom, handing her a box of tiramisu I picked up from Il Pompi.

"Grazie, cara. Call me Elenora." Elenora kisses both of my cheeks. "I'm so glad to finally meet you. And not just watch my son watch you at Angelina's." She laughs, clapping her hands together.

Lorenzo winces.

Claudia throws an arm around Lorenzo's shoulders. "This is going to be so much fun." Turning to me, she kisses my cheeks. "It's good to see you again. Come, let me take your coat." She pulls me toward the formal living room, taking my coat and scarf in the process.

Claudia sits in an armchair as I perch on the edge of the sofa.

"Get comfortable, Mia. Really, it's casual tonight." Claudia says, tucking her feet underneath her.

"Thanks," I sink back into the plush sofa.

The doorbell rings.

"Who's that?" Lorenzo asks, walking toward the door.

"No, I got it!" Claudia darts up and practically knocks Lorenzo down as she beelines for the door.

Elenora beams, her hands clasped in front of her waist.

"Who is it?" Lorenzo asks his mom.

"You'll see." She winks.

"Mama Elenora, thank you for the dinner invitation." Sandro walks into the room, glancing hesitantly at Lorenzo. "Ciao, Enzo. Mia." The corner of his mouth flips up in an almost-smile.

Lorenzo's mouth presses into a thin line, his hands clenching into fists. "You and my sister?"

Claudia looks at me, her eyes pleading for intervention

Standing up, I slip an arm around Lorenzo's waist, digging my fingers into his side. "Hi Sandro." I smile.

"Ciao Mia." He brushes a kiss against my cheek.

Lorenzo tenses next to me and I grip his hip harder.

"I'm so happy you could make it, Sandro. Have a seat. Dinner will be served shortly." Elenora takes Sandro's hands in hers and kisses both of his cheeks. "Lorenzo, drinks please." She tilts her head toward the wet bar.

Lorenzo nods, his jaw still tight. "What would you like?"

"Seriously?" Sandro asks him.

Lorenzo snorts and nods, moving toward the bar.

"Mia, I hear Enzo is coming to New York with you." Sandro says.

"Yes, for Christmas."

"And maybe staying longer?"

"You'll have to ask him about his plans."

Sandro's eyes scan mine, a grin shadowing his mouth. "I suppose I will."

Claudia perches on the armrest of Sandro's chair, dipping her head to whisper in his ear.

"You'll like this one." Lorenzo hands me a glass of wine, kissing my temple. "You tasted it in Tuscany."

He passes Sandro an Americano and the two of them clink glasses, some of the strain between them evaporating.

The conversation shifts to holiday plans and traditions as we engage in conversation.

"We'll have to double date before you guys leave." Claudia grins.

"Yes please!" I agree.

When dinner is served, Elenora sits at the head of the table, listening attentively and beaming with pride as she watches Lorenzo and Claudia joke around.

She piles second servings on mine and Sandro's plates. Lorenzo picks at my plate, helping to finish the extra serving without it looking obvious. My heart swells in gratitude at his intervention.

"You're good for him, Mia." Elenora smiles, covering my hand with hers.

"He's good for me too."

# 34

# LORENZO

"Just come, Claudia. I found the one. It's perfect."

She squeals and I know, without even seeing her, that she's jumping up and down. "I'll be right there. Don't move."

Staring at the flawless diamond ring pressed between my finger and thumb, I know it's the one. It's perfect for Mia. But, a second opinion never hurt, and no one knows jewelry like my sister.

"It's a beautiful ring. Stunning." Our family jeweler, Maria, smiles. "She must be a very special woman, Enzo."

"She is."

Jesu, I must be crazy to propose. I've only known Mia for a handful of months but this feels right. She's the woman for me and as we begin our life in America together, I want to start our journey as a true couple.

I want to promise myself to her for forever.

"I'm here." Claudia rushes in the gioielleria, a cold breeze trailing through the open door. "Oh my God. It's gorgeous," she exclaims, plucking the ring from my fingers. Holding it up to the light, she turns it from side to side. "It's perfect for her."

"You really think so?" Some of my nerves evaporate at my sister's approval.

"A hundred percent." She grins at me, wrapping her hand around my upper arm and resting her head against my shoulder. "And she's perfect for you. I'm really proud of you, Enzo."

"Thank you for coming. Your opinion means a lot."

"Trust me, this is the diamond."

"Maria, I'll take it."

"Excellent. Platinum band?" Maria asks.

"Of course."

"What size?"

Ah shit. *How could I forget to learn her ring size?*

"Six." Claudia says.

"What? How do you know that? Are you sure?"

"Yes, I knew you'd need my help."

Laughing in relief, I shake my head. "Thank you."

"You're welcome. You can repay me by taking me to lunch."

"I'd love to," I agree, opening my wallet and pulling out a debit card. "You can tell me all about Sandro."

Sliding it over the Maria, Claudia frowns. "I've never seen that card before."

"It's my personal savings."

"From your racing and the crappy summer jobs Papa forced us to work?"

"Exactly."

"Why are you using that card?"

I shrug. "It's important for me to buy the ring with money I earned. It doesn't feel right to start our life together on the backs of Mama and Papa's hard work, you know?"

Claudia nods, a smile flickering over her mouth. "I know. Trust me, she's going to fall in love with it."

———

WALKING INTO GHIACCIO, I spot Sandro at the bar, watching an AS Roma game.

"Enzo." Sandro stands from the barstool.

"My sister?" I bang my fist on the bar. "Two Peroni," I tell the bartender over my shoulder before glaring at my best friend.

"I know." He holds up a hand. "I should have told you."

"That would have been a good fucking place to start."

"Watch it, Enzo. This thing, all of it, is between Claudia and me. And while I admit I should have told you when I started to have feelings for her, when I wanted to act on them, I don't need your fucking permission. Or your approval."

The bartender sets two beers down in front of us. Picking mine up, I take a long pull, eyeing Sandro. He scowls at me, his jaw ticking. He's serious. "You treat her right?"

"Like a goddamn princess." He takes a pull of his beer, his eyes never leaving mine.

"It's for real?" He knows what I'm really asking: could you marry her?

"I love her."

I choke on my beer. "You love her? You barely know her!"

"Right, because you know Mia so fucking well you're planning on making her Mrs. Barca."

"You tell her yet?"

"You think it's too soon?" At the flicker of nerves in his tone, I grip the back of my neck and shake my head. Damn Sandro, he really loves my sister. And as much as I want to throttle him for not telling me, he's right. He doesn't need my permission or approval. And I would throttle any guy Claudia dated that wasn't willing to stand up to me and fight for her.

Because she's worth it.

And Sandro knows it.

"No, I don't think it's too soon."

"Me either." He flips his chin toward me. "You got a ring?"

"Yeah." I grin, pulling Mia's ring from my pocket and opening the box.

"Wow. Enzo, it's beautiful. She's going to love it."

"You'll be my best man?"

Sandro turns to me, clapping a hand on my shoulder. "I'd be honored." He gestures to the bartender. "Two shots."

"What are we celebrating?"

Sandro nods to the TV screen. "Roma's winning."

"Fuck off." I laugh, picking up the shot glass.

"Congrats, Enzo."

"Same to you, brother."

# 35

# MIA

The delicious aromas of cinnamon and nutmeg, of apple and pumpkin, of all the traditional goodness of a homemade Thanksgiving dinner waft around the Franchetti's apartment.

Gianluca has outdone himself.

Lexi bounces on her toes, placing a chocolate turkey next to each place setting at the table.

*Where did she even find them?*

"Expat grocery store," she answers my unasked question.

"How do you do that?"

"What? Read your mind?"

I nod.

"Your emotions flit across your face," Paola answers. "Your feelings, your thoughts, opinions… you don't hide your emotions as well as you think you do."

*Really?*

*How the hell did I manage to hide my food issues for so long?*

"Don't misunderstand me," Paola continues. "You're a

very private person, Mia. But when something surprises you, or confounds you, it's right there on your face."

"You wrinkle your forehead," Lexi adds.

"Oh," I say.

*Is that how Maura always seems to know how I'm feeling without me saying it?*

"It's not a bad thing," Lexi continues. "It just means I know you better than most people because I'm the best roomie you've ever had and you're going to miss me so much when you go back to New York. You'll probably cry for weeks." She fixes me with a stare. "Don't be embarrassed. I expect nothing less from you."

Rolling my eyes, I grin. "I'm sure." But I am going to miss her. A lot.

"Aw, Petunia. Don't cry!" Lexi pulls me into a one-arm hug as tears prick the corners of my eyes.

Damn it.

"Here, have a turkey." She passes me a piece of chocolate.

Laughing, I unwrap the chocolate and hand it out to Paola. She breaks off a piece and pops it into her mouth.

"Now, Paola, tell us again how we're your best, most favorite exchange students ever," Lexi starts folding napkins.

Paola drapes a hand over her heart, blinking furiously. "I just don't know how I'm going to exist once you leave, Lexi. I can't imagine a day without you in it. How will I ever enjoy a caffé again without your incredible latte art? How will I manage to get dressed without your expert fashion advice? How?"

"I know it will be difficult, but somehow, some way, you'll manage without me." Lexi says seriously.

Silence hovers over the kitchen as we all stare at each other, tears collecting in all of our eyes.

"You're not drinking in there, are you?" Gianluca calls out from his station at the stove.

The moment erupts and the three of us burst into laughter.

---

"Woo! Now that's a turkey!" Lexi cheers as Gianluca sets down a large, succulent turkey in the center of the dining table. "Well done, Gianluca!"

"It's my first Thanksgiving," he beams.

"Do you know how to carve it?" Lexi asks, skeptically.

"Of course I do."

"Another first," she whispers to me.

Paola snorts.

Next to me, Lorenzo chuckles, draping his arm along the back of my chair. Lexi's date, Scott, an American guy from her history class — who, she assured me, is not engaged — stands and offers to help.

"Okay," I glance around the table, "before we begin, let's all say one thing we're most grateful for this year."

"Yay! I love this game. I'll start." Lexi scoots her chair closer to the table. "This year, I'm most grateful to have had the opportunity to come to Italy and meet all of you." She smiles sweetly.

"I'm most grateful that even though we're abroad, we get to watch football today," Scott says, looking at Lorenzo, Gianluca, and Paola. "Real football, not soccer."

Silence. Oh wait, he's for real.

"I'm most grateful that," Paola pauses and takes Gianluca's hand, "we're most grateful to announce that we're having a baby!"

"What?" I laugh, throwing my arms around Paola.

"Oh my God!" Lexi exclaims.

"Auguri!" Lorenzo congratulates them.

"This is so exciting!" I gush.

"I know." Paola nods, happy tears tracking her cheeks.

"Don't cry, love." Gianluca kisses her hand.

"When did you find out?" I ask.

"Two nights ago," Gianluca says.

"This is the best Thanksgiving surprise ever!" Lexi cheers.

Scott mutters congratulations and helps himself to turkey.

Leaning over my chair, Lexi whispers in my ear, "No wonder he's single."

I snort.

Everyone piles their plates high with turkey, candied yams, stuffing, cranberry sauce, and cornbread.

Chewing a bite of turkey and stuffing, panic claws up my throat. The amount of food on my plate taunts me, expanding with each blink. It's too much food. Too many calories. Too many carbohydrates.

*Why is everyone looking at my plate? Do they know?*

Chatter buzzes in my ear.

I need to go to the bathroom.

Now.

Just as I'm about to push away from the table, Lorenzo's hand lands on my knee, sliding up to grip my thigh. I exhale, turning toward him.

He centers me without even knowing it.

"I never told you what I'm most grateful for," he whispers in my ear.

"What?"

"You. I love you, Mia."

"I love you too, Lorenzo."

# DECEMBER

# 36

# LORENZO

The next week passes in a blur as I finalize my preparations and arrangements for New York.

It's incredible how much my life has changed in a few short months.

No more wild nights or gambling sprees in Sanremo or digs.

Since meeting Mia, my perspective has shifted, my priorities have changed.

"Pronto?" I answer my ringing cell phone, taking a seat at a back table in Angelina's.

"Lorenzo Barca?" An American accent asks.

"Yes."

"This is Joe Esposito, your brother Anthony passed along your contact information."

"Oh? Ciao, Joe."

"I wanted to connect with you because Anthony says you're moving to New York. He and I were roommates in college and go way back. At first, I didn't think he was serious, but I looked you up, and man, you've got really impressive statistics. And F1 experience under your belt."

I clear my throat. *What is going on? Who is this guy?*

"I'm sorry, Joe. I don't understand…"

"I manage a racing team here in New York. We're looking for drivers. I'm going to email you the information and if you're interested, well, I'd love to sit down and talk once you're in town."

My heart rate thuds in my temples, my mouth growing dry.

Is he serious?

"Really?" I blurt out.

Joe laughs. "Really. We have a new sponsor and are looking to go F1 this season. It won't be easy. A lot of hours, training, preparation. But with the right driver, we're willing to throw our full support behind the operation. Maybe you've heard of us, Metrix Group."

Jesu.

"You partnered with Alfa Romeo last year."

"Exactly."

"Wow. I, I don't know what to say. I'd love to sit down and talk."

"Great, I'll send you some information. Give me a call when you're in the city."

"Absolutely. Grazie. Grazie mille." Hanging up the phone, I glance around Angelina's.

But it's late, the restaurant is closed, and I'm the only one here.

Except for the faces staring back at me from the old photographs lining the walls.

Generations of Barcas.

Mama was right.

Go back to the basics, to family, and my fortune will change.

I wonder if Papa is looking down at us all, laughing his ass off.

Not only did he safeguard his legacy from Benito by issuing a revised will at a later date, but he also strengthened the bond between Mama, Claudia, and me. And he gave us Anthony.

Tonight was my last shift at Angelina's, the family restaurant I never cared for and often resented.

But now, it's bittersweet to hang up my apron.

Now, when I glance at the patio, I see Mia's smile for the first time.

In the kitchen, I remember all the times I chopped vegetables standing next to Mama.

In this room, all the dinners my family had seated around a table, Papa giving Claudia and me our first taste of wine.

So many of my best memories, my happiest moments, have been right here in this tiny restaurant that six months ago, I never thought about.

Everything is changing.

And everything is exactly as it should be.

*Family. Family. Family.*

My fingers tremble as I stare at the keypad on my phone.

Jesu. I clench my hand into a fist to steady my nerves.

I need a drink.

No. That's not the way to do this.

This has to be right.

Perfect.

Like her.

She's my family.

Taking a deep breath, I pull the small box from my pocket and pop the lid. My breath catches in my throat as I stare at the diamond.

I never cared much for traditions until I met Mia.

Now, I want to do everything the right way.

Be the man Mama and Papa raised me to be.

Honor my wife.

Fucking worship her.

Closing the box, I exhale.

It's 7:00PM in New York.

Dialing the number, I hold the phone to my ear.

"Hello?" he answers on the fourth ring.

My blood runs hot and cold through my veins.

"Mr. Petrella. Ciao. My name is Lorenzo and I'm in love with your daughter."

# 37

# MIA

S topping on the Sant'Angelo Bridge, I pause to stare at the line of bridges crossing the Tiber.

To breathe in the day, and drink in the moment, and reflect.

Just weeks ago, my life changed on this bridge.

The love of my life stopped his bright red car in a rainstorm.

He looked at me through sheets of rain and blusters of wind and demanded I slide into the passenger seat of his car.

Anger and desire and pure need radiated from his eyes, keeping me speechless and frozen to the bridge.

I remember the smell of his skin, the heat of his touch, the raw honesty in his eyes as he drove me home.

They blazed as he undressed me, drinking in my body, making me feel beautiful. And worthy.

Two things I always feel when I'm with him.

Grinning, I walk home, enjoying the ordinary sights and regular landmarks that have seamlessly woven into my life over the past four months. Leaving Italy is bittersweet but I'm taking the best part of my Italian experience home with me.

I know I've changed. I came to Rome to shed Ballerina Mia, to find myself, to grow into a woman worthy of my mother's dreams.

It was hard and challenging and some days, I thought I would break.

But it was also exhilarating, and freeing, and beautiful.

Four months.

The college pact.

My whole life is different.

Pulling open the green door to the Franchetti's apartment, I jump in surprise.

"Morning, Petunia," Lexi greets me, picking at a cornetto. "I've been waiting for you."

"Why?"

"Because we have officially finished our final exams. And are leaving in a week." She rolls her eyes. "So there is nothing left for us to do but celebrate. Don't you think?" She licks a glob of chocolate off her knuckle.

"I'm going to miss you, Lex. What did you have in mind?"

"Well, here's where it gets interesting."

"What?" I ask slowly as a grin spreads across her face.

"You have a date tonight."

"I do? Lorenzo didn't mention anything."

"That's because I'm the Master of Ceremonies today. Or is it Mistress of Ceremonies? Mistress is so much better. God, I'm going to miss eating dessert for breakfast." She smacks her lips.

"What's the event?"

"You'll see." She glances at her watch. "You have ten minutes to shower and get ready."

"Wait what?"

"And read this." She hands me a folded-up piece of paper, hustling me to the bathroom. "Now shower so we can begin."

Closing the bathroom door, I turn on the water and open the note.

*Mia,*

*As your semester in Rome comes to an end, I'd like to mark your time here by celebrating your bravery, your courage, and all the challenges you've overcome. Your trust in me, in our relationship, and in yourself humbles me.*

*I've arranged for you and Lexi to get into some fun—and probably trouble—this afternoon. Humor Lexi. Let her take you around the city and participate in today's festivities. Here's a clue for your first stop: "Beauty awakens the soul to act."*

"Dante." *What is going on?*

Grinning, I exhale.

I'm even learning to appreciate surprises.

---

"A PARRUCCHIERA? REALLY?" I ask Lexi thirty minutes later as we stand outside a beauty salon.

"Yes, really. Your man thinks your beauty is connected to your soul. Or something." She scrunches her eyes, probably trying to remember the Dante quote. "Whatever, we're going home with new looks, lady. We are new people here. More confident, stronger, fun versions. Well," she squeezes my arm, "at least you are. I'm just along for the ride." She ushers me into the hair salon.

Lexi greets the receptionist, speaking in hushed tones.

Too hushed for me to catch.

But I'm not freaking out. I'm not.

"Just trust me, okay, Mia?"

Recalling the night before I left for Italy, the way I studied my reflection in the mirror as Emma packed my suitcase, I remember hating my stick straight hair, my pale complexion.

Change hasn't disappointed me yet.

"Okay."

"Good. Sit down." She motions toward a chair. "Don't worry. I'm getting my hair done too."

I sit where she gestures, smiling in the mirror when my eyes connect with the man who is going to cut my hair. "Ciao, my name is Michele. Don't worry, cara. I've got it all under control," he says, running his fingers through my hair.

"Okay."

---

"You look hot!"

"I have new hair." I stare at myself in the mirror, my mouth literally hanging open. "And you have no hair!"

"Ha! Short is the new long." Lexi twirls her new bob, soft waves framing her face. "But let's talk about you. I'm loving the side bangs and the layers. The highlights do so much for you. You look so much more…vibrant."

"Right?"

"Totally. New hair for the new year."

"New hair for the new year." I repeat, staring at my reflection.

My boring, plain Jane brown hair has been cut into an array of layers that add volume and life to my normally limp strands. Ribbons of chestnut and mocha and caramel paired with a low sweeping side bang create an allure of mystery I've never had before. And I love it.

My eyebrows are shaped and angled perfectly over my

eyes, which somehow appear larger with my new 'do. My nails and toes are buffed and polished pink.

I'm transformed.

A laugh spills from my lips as Lexi bumps her hip against mine. "See? I'm totally trustworthy, so don't try and fight me on our next stop." She hands me another folded note.

*"Segui il tuo corso, e lascia dir le genti."*

*"Follow your own road and let the people talk."*

"Dante again."

"You don't really have to do this, but I want to. So I'm dragging you along with me for support. Lorenzo agreed to incorporate this stop because I begged him, but he made me swear I won't peer pressure you." She rolls her eyes. "So, you decide."

Following her around the corner, we push through a door into —

"A freaking tattoo parlor!"

"Isn't this fun?" Lexi exclaims, pushing me into a chair. She pulls open a look book and comments on images she "truly loves" or "totally despises."

"That's hot," she points to a picture of a ripped guy with ink swirling up his side. It's suspiciously similar to Lorenzo's.

When the tattoo artist calls her name, I surprise both of us by standing up with her.

# 38

# LORENZO

"Slow down," Claudia warns, eyeing my third Negroni.

"Shit, I'm just nervous, you know?" I clutch my glass between my fingers like a life vest.

"Why? You seemed so calm when you bought the ring."

"I'm not nervous for me; I'm nervous for Mia. What if this is too much for her? She hates surprises."

"I bet she likes this one."

"Her dad thinks we're moving at lightning speed. He kept pointing out how young Mia is."

"But he gave you his blessing." My sister sips her cocktail, quirking an eyebrow over the rim.

"True. Do you think I'm rushing it? I can wait until we're settled in America. Or after she graduates."

"Enzo, what do you want?"

"I want to marry Mia. Be with her. Make her mine for always."

Claudia smiles, her eyes tearing up. "So?"

"So tonight's the night. I want to do this the right way. When we step on that plane, we'll be starting the next chapter of our lives together."

"True and you're overthinking it."

I snort, taking a gulp of my drink.

She squeezes my shoulder. "Relax. I'm just saying, Mia loves you. If you think this is right, then why are you so nervous about it?"

"I just…want to be enough for her."

"Enzo," Claudia covers my hand with hers on top of the bar, "you are. Trust me, Mia feels the same way about you."

"That's crazy," I scoff. "She's perfect."

"Yes, for you. Now let's look at the shiny ring again."

Pulling the box out of my pocket, I slide it across the bar to my sister. She opens it and sighs. "She's going to love it."

And I'm going to love her.

# 39

# MIA

I can't believe I got a freaking tattoo.

And changed my hair.

And am walking into the restaurant to meet Lorenzo for dinner like a badass.

I can't explain it, but I feel … more. Wrapped up in a self-assuredness, a comfortableness in my own skin that always seemed like a foreign concept.

Rocking thick black tights with ankle boots, thank you Lexi, and a black mini-skirt, I pull the cuffs of my coat over my fingers and take a deep breath.

Clutching Lorenzo's final note to me, I immediately recognize the quote from Dante's *Il Paradiso*.

*"Sei 'l'amor che move il sole e l'altre stelle.'"* You are *"the love that moves the sun and other stars."*

A shiver runs down my spine as I reread the words.

Stepping onto the patio, there's a secret in the air. Whispers of enchantment wrap around me like a blanket and my breath lodges in my throat.

Tiny lights twinkle in the bare branches of old stone pine trees like fireflies. Icy tendrils sweep through the air as a fire pit burns bright next to the table, chasing the frost away. A wrought-iron gate wraps around the patio, separating the restaurant from ancient Rome like a great time divider. Below the patio, the ruins unfold, white stone glistening in the moonlight.

It's breathtaking. Surreal.

Lorenzo's back is to me as he stares across the wonder of Ancient Rome. His hands wrap over the top of the gate, his muscles rolling beneath his coat as he shifts his weight. He turns as I make my way to the table, as if he senses my presence. When his eyes meet mine, a slow smile works its way across his lips.

"You found me."

"I did," I agree, holding up the note he left for me. "I had the best day." I step closer, taking Lorenzo's hand in mine. "No one has ever done anything like that for me before. Thank you."

His eyes glisten as he leans down and brushes a kiss across my lips. "You're welcome, bellezza. Always." His fingers touch the ends of my hair. "You look beautiful. But you always do. Wine?" He indicates the bottle already decanted on the table.

"Sure."

"Are you cold?" He picks up a wool blanket that hugs the back of my chair and wraps it around my shoulders.

Shivering, I'm not sure if it's from the cold or the look in Lorenzo's eyes. "Thank you." I smile, sliding into my chair, and glancing around.

"We're the only people out here." I look back to Lorenzo.

"We are."

"Another one of your surprises? This is pretty cool."

"It is, isn't it?"

A waiter appears next to our table and places down plates of appetizers: bruschetta, calamari, caprese salad.

"You look incredibly sexy." I grin, drinking in his dark jeans, the cream sweater peeking out of the collar of his navy cashmere coat. A light shadow coats his cheeks and chin, his hair expertly styled. But his eyes, they're mesmerizing. Serious and bright and … hopeful. "Lorenzo, what's going on?"

"Dig in." He nods toward the appetizers, loading his plate with a sampling.

I spear a piece of mozzarella and a tomato onto my plate and nibble. My stomach is in knots, butterflies fluttering up and down my ribcage.

"You're very quiet." He places a hand on mine.

"You're very…serious. Is everything okay?"

Lorenzo chuckles, "I was trying to wait until dessert but I'm too nervous."

"About what?"

"I was going to do this differently, but I guess it's all part of our story."

"What's going on?"

"I have one more quote for you."

"Dante?"

"Not quite." His expression earnest, his eyes serious, he quotes,

>*"Blessed be the day, and the month, and the year,*
>     *and the season, and the time, and the hour, and the moment,*
>     *and the beautiful country, and the place where I was joined*
>     *to the two beautiful eyes that have bound me:*

*and blessed be the first sweet suffering*
    *that I felt in being conjoined with Love,*
    *and the bow, and the shafts with which I was pierced,*
    *and the wounds that run to the depths of my heart.*

*Blessed be all those verses I scattered*
    *calling out the name of my lady,*
    *and the sighs, and the tears, and the passion:*

*and blessed be all the sheets*
    *where I acquire fame, and my thoughts,*
    *that are only of her, that no one else has part of."*

MY BREATH CATCHES in my throat. "Petrarch. That's from *Il Canzoniere*, Sonnet 61. It was one of Mom's favorites."

Lorenzo nods. "I'm so grateful for you, Mia. I love you. I think I've loved you since the first night I saw you sitting at Angelina's; I just didn't know it then. These past four months have been the best months of my life. So much has happened, a lot has changed, but as we make this next move, I want you to know that I'm all in.

I want us to mark the start of this journey as more than just boyfriend-girlfriend. I know you still have to finish school, and this is happening fast, but I know in my heart that I want to spend the rest of my life waking up and going to sleep next to you. And when you're ready, I want to call you my wife. Marry me, Mia."

*Marry him?*

My heart explodes in my chest, surprise rocking through me.

"Yes." I nod, tears already slipping past my eyelids. "Yes, Lorenzo, a thousand yeses. I love you too."

He slides a beautiful diamond onto my ring finger. It glitters and sparkles and takes my breath away. I look up at Lorenzo, but he's no longer sitting in his chair. Instead, he's kneeling by my side, clasping my fingers in his.

Standing, Lorenzo kisses me, his arm entwining my waist. His kiss swallows me whole; it absorbs my desires, strengthens my trust, eradicates my fears, extinguishes my uncertainty.

His kiss binds me to him and shows me our future.

Together.

# 40

## LORENZO

"You ready for this?" Mia asks as the wheels of our plane touch down in New York.

"I can't wait for this."

"We're meeting my friends on January 7." She holds out her hand, studying her ring. "They're going to die."

"Have you told them yet?"

"Is that a real question?"

"What did they say?"

"There was a lot of shouting. We're all chatting tomorrow on Google Hangout."

"I can't wait to meet them."

"They're going to love you."

"What about your dad?"

"I think he will too. Eventually."

I laugh, kissing the back of her hand. "You really believe this?" My thumb swipes across the fresh ink lining her inner wrist.

"With all of my heart."

*Sogno con occhi aperti.*

*I dream with open eyes.*

She does. She dreams beautiful dreams. And she's made all of mine come true. Even the ones I didn't know I had.

Mia Petrella has changed everything for me.

"I finally understand what Dante and Petrarca were always going on and on about in their poems."

"Oh yeah?" Mia quirks an eyebrow as the seatbelt sign flashes off.

Passengers stand and reach into the overhead storage bins.

"Si. You're my Beatrice. My Laura. The one that makes my life make sense. You've given me everything, Mia."

She smiles, her face transforming. "We're home, Lorenzo."

---

EXCITED GREETINGS, flowers, and signs welcome us as we exit immigration to the Arrivals corridor.

"Daddy!"

Mr. Petrella looks up. When he spots his daughter, a huge smile crosses his face, and he raises a hand in greeting. "Amelia! Welcome home!"

Next to him, a petite blonde grins.

Mia lunges forward and collapses against her father as he pulls her into his embrace.

"I've missed you," he whispers.

"I'm home now," she says.

Mr. Petrella squeezes Mia's shoulders as he kisses the top of her head. He steps back and sizes me up in the traditional way that father's check out their daughter's dates. Or in this case, fiancé.

"Lorenzo," he extends his hand.

"Mr. Petrella, it's a pleasure to meet you." I shake his hand. "In person."

He studies me for several seconds that stretch like life-times. My heart sputters in my chest and I freeze, suddenly scared that this man will find me lacking for his little girl.

And he'd be right.

But damn if I won't try to be enough for her. Always.

Mr. Petrella clears his throat and smiles. It's like a glacier melting; the atmosphere transforms. He pulls me into an awkward hug. "Congratulations. Call me Frank."

Claire clasps Mia's hand, glancing between Mia and me. "It's beautiful. We're so happy for you."

I breathe out a shaky breath, relieved to have passed a test I never thought I'd care about. Drinking in Mia's shining face, her father's sincerity, and Claire's warm smile, I thank my new family for inviting me to New York for Christmas.

The airport bustles around us, holiday music plays in the background, heavy jackets and thick scarves pass by in hordes, but when I look into Mia's eyes, we are the only two people in the entire airport, in the whole world.

And I'm finally home.

# 41

## MIA

"Show us the ring!" Emma shrieks, her face filling my screen.

I hold my hand up to the camera and the girls yell and cheer wildly.

"It's so sparkly!"

"Damn, now that's a rock!"

"I can't believe you're engaged!"

"Tell us everything about the proposal."

"Did he get down on one knee?"

Grinning, I ask, "Do you want to meet him?"

The cheering fills my bedroom as Lorenzo laughs. Rolling over onto his stomach, he scoops me into his side and positions the laptop on my bed until his face fills the screen.

"Buona sera, ragazze."

"Oh my God. Just keep talking!" Lila fans herself.

"Do you have any brothers?" Emma jokes.

"Actually —" Lorenzo starts but Maura's groaning interrupts him.

"Emma, tell him you're joking."

"I kid. I kid." Emma grins, fiddling with her bangs. "We're just really happy to meet the Italiano in person."

Lorenzo looks at me and I shrug.

"You know, Mia is sometimes meh; she glosses over the important details. Lorenzo, tell us how you proposed." Maura demands.

"Did you get down on one knee?" Lila asks.

"Did you ask Frank first?" Emma wonders.

Lorenzo chuckles, leaning closer to the computer screen. "What do you know about Dante and Petrarca?"

"Keep talking."

"I'm already swooning."

'The poets?"

Lorenzo glances at me over his shoulder. "This could be awhile."

"You have no idea."

---

CHRISTMAS MORNING IS different this year.

Mainly, because when I roll over in bed, Lorenzo is sleeping soundly beside me. Brushing a kiss across his temple, I slip out of bed and pull on my robe.

Turning slowly in my bedroom, my entire childhood unfolds around me. Dance awards and trophies line my bookshelves. Less than a year ago, they were the reason I woke up in the morning, and now, they belong to an entirely different phase of my life. One I recall but don't really remember.

Framed photographs sit on my dresser. One of me with my parents, one with Mom holding me as a baby, her eyes shining with so much love and pride, another from Dad's wedding to Claire, and then, the last photo Lila, Emma,

Maura, and I took before I left for Rome. Claire must have updated the frame while I was gone.

Picking up the frame, I study myself in the picture. It's hard to believe that just four months ago, I existed as a shadow. Pale, gaunt, and so thin I looked sick. Since this photo was taken, I've gained seven pounds and even though it's sometimes heart-wrenching to watch the numbers on the scale increase, I do look healthier.

And happier.

Padding downstairs to the kitchen, I text the girls Merry Christmas.

"Merry Christmas Daddy." I step into the kitchen, already breathing in the fresh pot of coffee Claire brewed.

As usual, Dad's sitting at the kitchen table, reading the paper, his mug of coffee in hand.

"Merry Christmas, Mia." He stands, kissing my cheek and preparing me a cup of coffee. "It's different this year, huh?" his eyes glance at the ceiling, upstairs, to where Lorenzo is still tucked in bed.

"Sure is."

"You're different," he hands me a mug.

"I am. You remembered." I raise my mug to him.

"Skim milk, no sugar, two spins of the spoon."

I grin, sliding onto my chair.

"I'm happy for you Mia." Dad sits down and slides the Arts section of the paper to me.

"Thanks Daddy. Me too."

For a moment, my past and present collide: me as a little girl sitting next to my dad on Sunday mornings, reading the comics and sipping chocolate milk while Mom dressed upstairs; me as a woman sitting next to my dad on Christmas morning, reading the paper and sipping coffee while my fiancé sleeps upstairs.

I stifle a giggle. Dad lowers his newspaper, giving me a knowing look over the top.

"Merry Christmas, Mia." Claire enters the kitchen, her robe cinched over her pajamas.

"Merry Christmas, Claire. Thanks for making coffee."

# JANUARY

## LORENZO

"Ten, nine, eight …" The countdown to the New Year rings out in the small, Italian restaurant.

Mia shines, her dark hair swept away from her face, her eyes glowing with happiness. Bouncing with each passing second, she tips her champagne flute toward me. "This is going to be the best year yet."

I grin, nodding, as Frank and Claire cheer, as Anthony and his girlfriend Stephanie hold noisemakers and don celebratory hats.

"Five, four …"

She leans up, her mouth colliding with my ear. "I love you."

"Three, two, one."

"Happy New Year!" the room erupts.

Pulling her into me, I kiss her hard as noisemakers echo and streamers float around us. Fireworks explode in the night sky as the first seconds of the New Year are celebrated throughout New York City.

"I love you more. I'll always love you best."

"Happy New Year." Frank clasps my shoulder, kissing the top of Mia's head.

"Happy New Year, brother." Anthony throws an arm around my shoulder as Stephanie kisses my cheek.

Glitter and confetti swirl around the room, crazy party hats and sunglasses strewn across tables, balloons cover the ceiling. Smiling faces and celebratory cheers echo and I wish I could freeze this moment.

Mia's squeal as Anthony lifts her up and spins her around.

Claire lovingly kissing Frank.

Stephanie's smile.

Surrounded by so much happiness and love as the most challenging year of my life comes to a close, I am grateful and excited for the future.

"What are you thinking about?" Mia asks.

"Nothing," I shake my head. "Just this moment, you know?"

"Yeah, it's like if you could freeze time and remember everything about right now, every single detail, every emotion you have, all the thoughts in your mind, and hold onto them forever, you would, right?"

"All I'll remember about this moment is: *'We were together. I forget the rest.'*"

"Dante?"

"Walt Whitman."

Mia bursts out laughing, music and poetry blending as I pull her into my arms and kiss her.

"Then I'll remember for the both of us," she whispers against my lips, kissing me back.

Her kiss.

Her.

The best way to start the New Year.

The best way to begin my life.

# EPILOGUE

**Eight Months Later - Mia**

"How do I look?"

"Petunia, is that a real question? You're already making me tear up." Lexi dabs underneath her eyes with a tissue.

"You look beautiful." Maura smiles at me through the reflection of my full-length mirror.

"Breathtaking." Lila agrees. "And, I'd like to thank you because this is the only bridesmaid's dress I think I can wear again." She smooths her hands down her frame.

I grin. "I'm glad you girl like it."

"You should; you picked them out." Emma rolls her eyes at Lila.

As Emma and Lila debate the merits of their bridesmaids' dresses, Maura fingers the crystal hair combs in my hair. "I love your something blue."

"Thank you. Lorenzo's mother gave them to me."

"She wore them on her wedding day too." Claudia smiles.

"They look beautiful in your hair. What's your something new?"

I point to the diamond studs in my ears. "A gift from Lorenzo."

"Naturally." Claudia laughs.

"That man is going to have you dripping in diamonds." Lexi grins.

"Claire lent me my something borrowed." I hold up my wrist where a diamond bracelet my dad gifted her on their wedding day shines.

"That was nice of her."

"We've gotten a lot closer these past few months. She's been amazing helping me plan this wedding. It's been nuts trying to coordinate everything."

"Yeah, well, not everyone gets married in the Italian Riviera." Maura grins.

"But, we're so grateful you did!" Lila rejoins our conversation, sipping on Prosecco.

"Seriously Mia, I don't even want to go to another wedding after this. And it hasn't even started." Emma laughs.

"I'm glad you all came."

"As if we'd miss your wedding day." Lila shakes her head. "You know, this trip gave Cade so much to look forward to. I'm so happy we're here."

"Me too." I squeeze her hand.

"Mia." My dad steps into the room where the girls and I are getting ready. He holds out a small box. "Your something old."

Tears dots the corners of Daddy's eyes as I accept the box. "Thank you." Opening it, my breath catches in my throat. A thin, delicate, diamond eternity ring sits inside. "This was Mom's."

Dad smiles, tears streaming down his cheeks. "I told myself I wouldn't cry this early."

"Ah, Frank, cut yourself some slack." Emma hands him a handful of tissues.

Dad laughs, dabbing his eyes and nodding. "This was Mom's wedding band. She'd want you to wear it."

Slipping it onto the ring finger of my right hand, I smile through my tears. "Thank you Daddy."

"Happy wedding day, baby girl."

A knock at the door has us all turning. "It's time." Claire smiles. "Mia, Lorenzo looks absolutely dashing."

"And I bet nervous." Claudia adds.

Claire nods and the girls laugh.

"You ready for this?" Dad asks, squeezing my hands.

"I can't wait for this."

---

**Epilogue - Lorenzo**

Pachelbel's "Canon in D" plays as Mia walks toward me.

Her father clasps her hand.

Murmurs fill the Church.

Mama dabs at her eyes with a handkerchief.

But all I see is Mia.

A beautiful, white lace gown hugs her curves, a veil trails down the center of her back, flower petals dance around her feet.

But the only thing I'll remember from this moment is her smile.

Radiant. Fulfilled. Happy.

A swell of emotion clogs my throat as Sandro squeezes my shoulder. "Breathe."

I nod. But I'm too overwhelmed by Mia's beauty.

When Frank places her hands in mine, I kiss her cheeks and squeeze her fingers.

"I love you." She breathes.

"Heavenly Father, we are gathered here today to witness the joining of two lives…" Father Michele begins.

Throughout the ceremony, my eyes are trained on Mia.

She's calm, sweet, and so incandescent, she rivals the sun.

"I now pronounce you husband and wife." Father Michele smiles. "You may kiss your bride."

Wrapping my arm around Mia's back, I hold her cheek, dip my head, and kiss my wife.

Cheering and clapping surround us.

Laughing, Mia pulls back, her eyes shining.

"I love you more, Mrs. Barca."

---

"I can't believe you're married." Sandro hands me a Negroni.

"I know." I glance around at the cocktail hour, the mingling of our wedding guests, our friends and family celebrating our union.

"Man, I want to retire here." Anthony takes a sip of his drink, staring at the sunset.

"Yeah, Santa Margherita Ligure is pretty special." I admit.

"Anthony, make him give you the keys to his new house. It's about five streets from here."

Anthony raises his eyebrows.

"Visit anytime you want, brother."

"I'm taking you up on that."

"Anytime." I repeat. "You and Stephanie should come to the Grand Prix in September."

"Hell yeah." Anthony agrees. "I'd love that."

"About time you race again." Sandro comments, leaning back against the bar.

"This has been some year." I agree, my mind wandering back to all the practices and trainings. "Mia's a nervous wreck but I'm pumped for the Italian Grand Prix."

"You should be." Anthony takes a sip of his drink. "It's one hell of an accomplishment. You should be proud."

"The only thing I'm proud of is convincing Mia to marry me. Excuse me gentlemen, my bride awaits." I hand Anthony my Negroni and meet Mia on the dance floor.

"Dance with me." I take her hand in mine.

"Today is perfect. It's more than I ever dreamed."

"You're more than I ever dreamed."

Twirling Mia around the dance floor once, twice, I tuck her into my embrace. Holding her close, I whisper in her ear.

"*Remember tonight, for it is the beginning of always.*"

"Dante." She breathes.

"Dante." I confirm. "Love you, Mia."

"Always, Lorenzo."

---

HOPE YOU LOVED Mia and Lorenzo's story! Get ready for Maura and Zack in *All the While* — a raw, emotional, brother's best friend romance coming July 16, 2o19.

Keep reading for a sneak peek.

Sign up here to learn when All the While is live!

# AN EXCERPT FROM ALL THE WHILE

**Maura**

I wasn't always promiscuous.

In fact, I never slept around until Adrian disappeared from my life.

Before that, I cared too much about his opinion, the values our parents raised us with, to ever have a slew of one-night stands. But when he stopped playing by the rules, I figured why the hell shouldn't I?

And that's how it started.

The drinking, the sex, the painful loneliness that eats pieces of my heart and gnaws at my soul. Even when I'm surrounded by people, with my entire team, laughing with my best friends, Emma, Lila, and Mia, I'm so alone it hurts to breathe in too deep.

Like if I do, I'll shatter the façade I'm trying so hard to keep up.

And so I drink.

Wine, Vodka, Tequila.

Anything to numb my body from absorbing the shock of

Adrian's loss. Anything to numb my mind from processing that he's gone, from addressing the anger I'm harboring over his death.

Because the truth is, I'm furious at my twin for leaving me behind.

How can you stay angry at a dead person when the rest of his world, those who loved him and grieve for him, placed him on a pedestal?

My mom can't mention his name without tears welling up in the corners of her eyes. My dad prefers to pretend that everything is fine.

And so I'm utterly alone.

Alone in my thoughts, alone in my missing, and definitely alone in my anger which, some days, threatens to consume me.

To embrace the numbing detachment I've come to rely on, I need to drink.

I need to inhale the calming sweetness of Marlboro Menthol Golds like no athlete before me ever has.

I need to have lots of deliciously mind-numbing sex with random men.

In the mornings that follow, I wash their scent off of my skin and pretend the night before never happened. And sometimes, if I'm really lucky, I can hardly remember the night at all.

The only thing I don't touch, never have, never will, is drugs.

Because as much as I miss my brother, I'm furious with him for taking his own life. Sure, he didn't intend to at the time. But isn't an overdose just as selfish as suicide?

I keep my grades up, smile politely at my professors, banter with my classmates. I attend practices on time, dig into each and every catch, my hair tucked into one of Adrian's old baseball caps, my sunglasses hiding the void in my eyes. And even though everyone knows something is wrong, something is off, no one can figure out what it is.

Until Zack.

Adrian's best friend.

---

Sign up to learn when *All the While* is live!

Add All the While to your TBR.

# WORKS CITED

This book references and discusses poetry from Dante Alighieri, Francesco Petrarca, and Walt Whitman. The following works were utilized:

Alighieri, Dante. 1265-1321. *The Divine Comedy*. Trans. John Ciardi. New York: Penguin Group. Electronic.

Alighieri, Dante. 1265-1321. *La Vita Nuova*. Trans. Mark Musa. New York: Oxford University Press, Inc., 1992. Print.

Petrarca, Francesco, Giacomo Leopardi, and Luigi Domenico Spadi. 1858. *Il canzoniere*. Firenze: A. Bettini.

Whitman, Walt. *Leaves of Grass*: The First (1855) Edition. New York: Penguin Books, 2005. Print.

# ACKNOWLEDGMENTS

Hello Readers!

So much thanks for so many wonderful people —

Regina Wamba at Mae I Design – you are awesome at your craft!! I love the covers for this series so much! Just looking at them makes me think of college and smile.

Melissa Panio-Peterson – A million thank yous for all of your time and support! Working with you is the best!

Patrick Hodges - Thank you for always being a sounding board and for proofing my books and catching all the typos I miss!

All the wonderful writers at Romance Author Mastermind 2018 – If it wasn't for all I learned from you awesome ladies, I wouldn't have revamped this series and I am so, so glad I did. Thank you for the insight, encouragement, and invaluable advice.

THANK YOU amazing bloggers! A special thank you to Ola, Chloe (bibliophilechloe), Sandra (cofffeeandbooks), and Alexis, Dana, Melanie, and Heather (a book nerd, a bookseller and a bibliophile) – your support is everything!

To all the readers – I hope this book encouraged you to reminisce about your college adventures – and loves! I am forever grateful.

To my home team – Tony, Aiva, Rome, and Luna – love you all the world. Always.

Happy Reading!

Xo,

Gina

# ALSO BY GINA AZZI

**The Kane Brothers Series:**

*Rescuing Broken* (Jax's Story)

*Recovering Beauty* (Carter's Story)

*Reclaiming Brave* (Denver's Story)

*My Christmas Wish*

(A Kane Family Christmas

+ *One Last Chance* FREE prequel)

**Finding Love in Scotland Series:**

*My Christmas Wish*

(A Kane Family Christmas

+ *One Last Chance* FREE prequel)

*One Last Chance* (Daisy's Story)

*This Time Around* (Coming September 2019)

**The College Pact Series:**

*The Last First Game (Lila's Story)*

*Kiss Me Goodnight in Rome* (Mia's Story)

*All the While* (Maura's Story)

*Me + You* (Emma's Story)

**Standalone**

*Corner of Ocean and Bay*

# ABOUT THE AUTHOR

Gina Azzi writes Contemporary Romance with relatable, genuine characters experiencing real life love, friendships, and challenges. She is the author of The Kane Brothers Series, The College Pact Series (re-launching summer 2019), and Corner of Ocean and Bay. All of her books can be read as stand-alones.

A Jersey girl at heart, Gina has spent her twenties traveling the world, living and working abroad, before settling down in Ontario, Canada with her husband and three children. She's a voracious reader, daydreamer, and coffee enthusiast who loves meeting new people. Say hey to her on social media or through www.ginaazzi.com.

For more information, connect with Gina at:

Email: ginaazziauthor@gmail.com
Twitter: @gina_azzi
Instagram: @gina_azzi
Facebook: https://www.facebook.com/ginaazziauthor
Website: www.ginaazzi.com

Or subscribe to her newsletter to receive book updates, bonus content, and more!

Made in the USA
San Bernardino, CA
13 May 2020